A Private Crime

A PRIVATE CRIME

by

Lillian O'Donnell

G. P. PUTNAM'S SONS
New York

G. P. Putnam's Sons
Publishers Since 1838
200 Madison Avenue
New York, NY 10016

Printed in the United States of America

Quality Printing and Binding by:
ARCATA GRAPHICS/KINGSPORT
Press and Roller Streets
Kingsport, TN 37662   U.S.A.

A Private Crime

Prologue

"Day and night they're marching in front of the house carrying plac- ards and chanting. They're trying to drive the boy and his family out of their home and your cops aren't doing anything about it!" Bernard Yost charged, his sonorous voice throbbing with emotion as though he were already addressing a jury.

"We've responded to every complaint," Captain Emmanuel Jacoby replied mildly as he turned the pages of the report in front of him.

"Oh, they go through the motions, sure. They show up; they disperse the demonstrators, and send everybody home. Then they leave. As soon as they're gone, the people come back out and start all over again."

Manny Jacoby spread out his pudgy hands in a gesture of futility. "What do you suggest?"

"You could lock up the demonstrators, charge them with disturbing the peace."

Jacoby, commander of the 20th Precinct, glanced over to Lieutenant Mulcahaney, head of the Fourth Homicide Division, one of the over- head units quartered in the Eighty-second Street station house. She said nothing, admiring the captain's equanimity. "Lock up a whole neigh- borhood?" he asked.

"If that's what it takes!" the lawyer, tall, dark, saturnine, thundered. "Unless you're not sure your men can handle the job," he added. Seeing Jacoby's round, hitherto pleasant face darken and sweat glisten in the deep creases of his forehead, Yost knew he had gone too far, so without further ado, he opened his briefcase and took out a piece of crumpled notepaper, smoothed it, and placed it in front of the captain.

"This was tied around a rock and thrown through the Hites' window."

Get out! Sons of Satan! Seeds of evil! You belong in hell. If you don't get out, we'll send you there. Burn forever!

"That tells me they're going to torch the house," Yost concluded.

Jacoby held the paper out to Norah Mulcahaney. She took it, read it, and impassively handed it back.

"Well, what are you going to do about it?"

"What do you want me to do?" Jacoby retorted.

"The least you can do is post a guard."

Jacoby didn't answer right away. The continuing hubbub in the squad room outside emphasized the silence in the small, cluttered, and overheated office. Though Captain Jacoby appeared to be considering the request seriously, Norah Mulcahaney didn't believe he was. Protection for a suspected criminal was far from unusual, but in this instance she found it repugnant and knew Manny Jacoby well enough to believe it was offensive to him, too.

"If you're afraid for your client's safety, why don't you get him to turn himself in?" Jacoby asked.

"Because he's innocent. Because he didn't do it," Yost stated smugly, and whereas up to now he had ignored Lieutenant Mulcahaney, in charge of the Hite investigation, he now challenged her directly. "You can't prove otherwise and you know it. You're hoping the neighbors' demonstrations will frighten my client into confessing."

Norah Mulcahaney was thirty-nine, a twelve-year veteran. She'd made detective within two years of joining the force, an achievement in itself, and shortly thereafter made sergeant. Except for a brief period during which she had formed and headed a Senior Citizens Squad, Norah had worked her entire career out of Homicide. She'd started with the elite Homicide North then, with the restructuring of the detectives division into zones, was assigned to the Fourth. Two years ago, having passed the lieutenant's exam, she'd been appointed to head the unit.

Norah was tall, five eight in stocking feet, and carried herself with quiet confidence. Having no need to attract attention, she dressed functionally. Today, she was wearing a light-gray pants suit with a sapphire-blue sweater. She used little makeup and pulled her glossy, dark-brown hair back severely, tied with a scarf that matched the sweater and brought out the deep blue of her eyes. Lines were beginning to show on her brow, around her eyes and mouth, but they were faint except in moments of stress and did not detract from her fine complexion.

Norah Mulcahaney had strong convictions, and she was known to speak her mind. But she was present at this interview at Manny Jacoby's behest as an observer and would not participate unless he indicated she should. So she retained her composure—high brow clear, dark-blue eyes steady, and the blunt, square chin firm, revealing nothing of what she felt.

She felt outrage and indignation and sorrow.

It seemed to Norah that the murders were growing not merely in numbers but in depravity, in heart-numbing contempt for the human condition. This one was particularly shocking. One of the worst she could remember.

At the beginning, the case had moved fast. It started with the victim's mother reporting her nine-year-old son, Pepe, missing. A search was instituted and it didn't take long to find the boy, his body mutilated and abandoned in the very tenement in which he'd lived. He had been hacked to death, the various body parts placed in black plastic bags and set to one side to be put out with the trash for pickup. It didn't take long for Norah and the squad to turn Raymond Hite, who lived next door and was just fourteen years old, as the only suspect. His parents appealed to Legal Aid for a lawyer and Bernard Yost was assigned. On his advice, young Hite stopped talking to the police.

His refusal to answer stymied them. Norah Mulcahaney admitted it. There was no physical evidence linking Hite to the victim, so there was nothing more the police could do. For five days now there had been no mention of the crime by the media. The case, though technically open, appeared to be destined to be pushed into the background and forgotten.

"I demand protection for my client—for the boy and for his family." Yost addressed himself to both Jacoby and Mulcahaney.

To function as a Legal Aid lawyer, one had to be committed to the concept that no matter how heinous the crime, the suspect was entitled to the best possible defense. Norah accepted that, the justice system was based on it, but she thought she detected a current of desperation under Yost's arrogance. Looking to Manny Jacoby, she got the nod.

"Don't worry, Counselor, we'll make sure he's okay. We're on our way now to pick him up."

That wasn't the kind of protection he'd been agitating for. "Why? On what evidence? The crack?"

In the search of the suspect's home a small amount of crack and the equipment for smoking it was found in Raymond Hite's closet. Deemed as of minor importance, it had been routinely sent to the lab.

"If you want to bust him for possession, go ahead. You know how fast I'll have him out."

"That won't be the charge," Norah told him quietly.

"What then? You've got no physical evidence that young Hite and the victim were ever in contact."

"We have now," she said.

"What? What've you got?"

Captain Jacoby intervened. "That will be disclosed at the proper time."

Yost scowled. He considered. "Let me talk to the boy and to his family, then we can set up a time and place for him to surrender."

The evidence on which the arrest would be made was saliva. Spit. His murderer had killed the nine-year-old child, then spit on him. A careful medical examiner had discerned the dried spittle on the child's left cheek, and by way of the seemingly irrelevant crack pipe, using DNA testing procedures, had matched it to Raymond Hite. The dreadful crime had been committed under the influence of crack and it was grim justice, Norah thought, that the drug should serve as the means by which the killer would be convicted.

"It's too late for that," Jacoby told the lawyer and then nodded to Norah Mulcahaney.

She got up and started for the door. This crime, like so many others recently, would not even have been committed, she thought, B.C.

Before crack.

Chapter ONE

It was Saturday, April 29th, the start of New York City's weekend-long celebration to commemorate the two hundredth anniversary of George Washington's inauguration as president on the steps of Federal Hall. A group of volunteers would reenact the ceremony and later the mayor, the governor, and the vice president were scheduled to review the parade of tall ships, before dining with other dignitaries at Gracie Mansion. A spectacular fireworks display on the East River off Wall Street, where Washington landed two hundred years ago, would mark the end of the first day's public festivities.

There would be private celebrations of the event as well, from simple picnics to lavish entertainments—rain threatened but did not dampen enthusiasm. Norah planned to spend the evening with Randall Tye. The television newsman and anchor could have gone to any and all of the official functions, but in deference to the private nature of their friendship, he planned a cookout on the terrace of his midtown penthouse from which the fireworks would be visible and invited Norah along with a few friends. She was eagerly looking forward to it.

In fact, Norah thought as she stood at her closet that morning trying to decide what she would wear that night, she was thinking a lot about Randall these days as he became an ever more important part of her life. Tye was more than a television journalist. He had his own talk show; he mingled with celebrities, and was a celebrity in his own right, a fact which had put Norah off when she first met him.

With his square, rugged face, wavy blond hair, and amber eyes, Tye would never be lost in a crowd, although he was not outstandingly handsome, either. He had charisma, a force of personality more powerful than mere looks. Randall was a hard worker and prepared his material with meticulous regard for accuracy, but it was the personal quality that put him at the top of his field.

Norah had not imagined any kind of relationship was possible between them, but he was instantly attracted to her and he was hard to resist. When Norah found out that the parties, the shows, the dinners to which he escorted her were all on the cuff, all trade-offs for a mention on Tye's show or at least for an attitude of goodwill when someone else mentioned them, she was disappointed. As a police officer, she couldn't accept handouts. As a private person, she considered them bribes. Randall explained it as part of the job, accepted procedure, but he respected Norah's viewpoint and promised that in the future their dates would be totally "uncontaminated."

He proposed marriage. He offered a partnership of love, companionship, and a careful separation of their professional lives.

"Try it and you'll like it," Randall Tye had urged.

She said no, but he wouldn't give up. He even accepted her refusal of premarital sex.

Norah caught herself daydreaming about Randall Tye during work. That had only happened once before, with the man she'd married—Joseph Antony Capretto. She had not thought it could happen again, certainly not after the way Joe had died. That was over four years ago and she couldn't forget, nor did she want to. The union with Joe had been complete and fulfilling. They shared everything including—and maybe superseding all else—The Job. Randall Tye argued for another way. He offered support without intrusion. Norah was beginning to wonder how long she could abide by the rules she herself had set down.

The atmosphere at the Two-Oh was almost festive when Norah arrived for work Saturday morning. A major percentage of the uniformed force would be assigned to crowd control for the next two days. Along with sanitation and other services the bill to the taxpayers for the pomp and pageantry was anticipated at $6.1 million. Two million people were expected to enjoy the events of the first day. The atmosphere was different from that of a visit by a foreign dignitary; on such occasions there was the danger of terrorist attack. Today, it would be all celebration and patriotic pride. There would be pickpockets out to work the crowds, some muggers, some drunks, and always the drug dealers, but the heavy crimes, specifically homicides, should be down.

According to the latest statistics a homicide occurred in New York City every five hours, but in the Fourth Zone the incidence had decreased. That was chance, of course, Norah knew. However, the solution rate was up, way up, and for that she and the squad could take credit.

"Morning, Lieut," Detective Simon Wyler greeted Norah. "Got a minute?"

"Sure. Come on in." She led the way into her office.

Wyler had just turned thirty. He had reached his present rank of Detective, First Grade, four years ago and transferred from midtown South two and a half years ago. He had become one of Norah's mainstays. He was six foot two, slim, jaunty, dapper. His dark, wavy hair swept back from a sharp peak; his nose was aquiline. He favored wide-brimmed fedoras and long, narrow topcoats. He was intelligent, low key, a good interrogator who didn't need to rely on physical intimidation. Norah frowned on her people allowing a situation to deteriorate to the point where force was required. That suited Wyler and so did the assignment to the Fourth. After stints at Safe and Loft, Community Relations, and a Narcotics Task force, Wyler had found his slot.

"About the Hite case, Lieut . . ."

Wyler and Julius Ochs had made the collar on the Monday. Norah had been present, along with additional RMP (Radio Motor Patrol) cars, not because supervision was necessary, but because the neighborhood situation was so extremely volatile. Both precautions had turned out to be unnecessary. When the men and women in the picket line saw the blue-and-white official cars and the unmarked vehicles belonging to the detectives lining up in front of the Hite building, they stopped chanting and parted ranks to let Detectives Wyler and Ochs through. When, after a short period, they emerged with the young suspect, his head bowed—in remorse, humiliation, or defeat—a low murmur rippled through the crowd. The police, particularly the two detectives flanking Raymond Hite, pretended not to be aware of the rumble. But even if they hadn't heard it, the emotion was palpable. It hung in the air like a heavy, clammy fog.

Norah watched from her car as Wyler and Ochs escorted the suspect out the front door of the dilapidated brownstone and down the steps from the stoop to the street. She wished Wyler and Ochs would move him along a little faster, get him into the safety of the police car, and drive away. At the same time, she knew that any indication of haste was to be avoided. It would suggest anxiety and stimulate and encourage action against him. So she could only wait, counting the steps that remained before they reached the car and the seconds it took to open the rear door and get him inside. As the doors shut, Norah breathed a sigh of relief. And then she heard it—a sound she did not at first recognize.

Applause. Cheers.

Some of the neighbors of West Ninety-third laughed, some cried, but all applauded.

The booking and arraignment had proceeded routinely. On Thursday morning, the 27th, Raymond Hite's case had been heard by the grand jury and the indictment handed down. A trial date was yet to be set.

"So? Has he made bail?" Norah asked. The judge, citing both the depravity of the crime and the feelings of the neighborhood, had set bail at $500,000. No one expected the Hites to raise it. If they did and the suspect was on the street, the problem of his safety, bad enough while he was in custody, would be exacerbated.

"No." Wyler replied.

"Well?"

"Three different people on the block now remember seeing the victim, Pepe, go into the Hite house by the back door. Ray Hite followed a few minutes after."

"These individuals were already interrogated in the canvass?"

"Right."

Their earlier silence had been based on fear. Norah knew that; so did every man and woman on the force. Everybody in the city was afraid— the old of the young, the whites of the blacks, the rich of the poor. Protection couldn't be guaranteed to every potential witness. Getting maimed or killed was a high price to pay for being a good citizen.

"What made you go back?" Norah asked.

"I had a hunch. Those three people looked to me like they were holding back," Wyler explained. "I made a note to try again if I got the chance."

The case would be made on the DNA evidence, Norah thought. This new testimony was circumstantial, but it would serve to bolster the other.

"Are they willing to appear in court?"

"They are."

"Good work, Simon."

By noon Norah and Ferdi Arenas were working on next month's chart. The way things were progressing, she'd have no problem getting away to change for Randall's cookout. They sent out for lunch and were breaking for a few minutes to eat it.

"What are you doing tonight?" she asked Ferdi.

"We got a neighbor to baby-sit and we're going to the concert in the park."

"Nice," Norah said and smiled. The bond between them was strong. Ferdi had been with her since her first command—the Senior Citizens Squad. She had been a sergeant then, and he a rookie, but the warmth of their friendship was based on more than the years together on the force. Each had lost a loved one to The Job—Norah, her husband; and Ferdi, the woman he'd intended to marry. After five years Ferdi had found the inner peace and the courage to love again. Now he was married and the father of twin girls and an infant son. He would have liked to help Norah find her way to new happiness, but he was shy about intruding into her personal life. It seemed to him that she had given him an opening.

"What are your plans?" he asked.

"Randall's having a cookout on his terrace." She looked at him expectantly.

"You like him, don't you?"

"Very much." She hesitated. "He's asked me to marry him."

"Oh." Ferdi hadn't expected anything like this. Did she want advice or just someone to listen?

"I don't know what to do," Norah blurted out as surprised as Ferdi. She hadn't meant even to mention the proposal. So she must be considering it more seriously than she'd realized herself. "I could resign . . ."

"Resign? From The Job? Turn in your shield?" Arenas was stunned.

"I don't think the marriage could work otherwise."

Stunned enough to overcome his reticence. "You love The Job! For sure the marriage wouldn't work if you gave it up. You tried that once before."

After Joe's death.

Her life was divided into before and after Joe's death. She remembered every detail of that day. Joe, then a captain, was working out of the office of the C of D (Chief of Detectives) in the Big Building, One Police Plaza. Norah was, as now, at the Two-Oh, though not in command. She was still a sergeant. They had been married six years and after a shaky period were finding each other again. That night they'd planned to eat out in a new and elegant restaurant near their home. Norah caught a squeal at the very end of her shift, one she could easily have passed on to the man who was scheduled to relieve her, but the details were intriguing; she wanted the case. So she called Joe to say she'd be late. Under the circumstances, Joe decided he might as well work late, too, and by the time he left his office, the streets around One Police Plaza were dark and nearly empty. As he entered the parking lot under the bridge where he kept his car, Joe Capretto heard a woman scream. He had interrupted a rape. The assailants and Joe went down. He was able to draw his gun, but before he could shoot, they were in their car and heading straight at him. He was caught in the undercarriage and dragged through the streets.

The funeral had been the department's way of showing respect for the slain officer, and was a consolation for Joe's mother, Emilia Capretto, and his seven sisters. For Norah it was merely an empty ritual. His killers had not been apprehended. She knew a massive investigation had been organized, but the two thugs had disappeared into the adjoining, tortuous maze of Chinatown. They would be found, Chief of Detectives Luis Deland promised the widow. Inspector James Felix, a friend of many years first to Joe and then to Norah, had been more honest and had added: sooner or later. That meant the police might have to wait till the perpetrators committed another, similar offense.

That was when Norah resigned, or tried to. Jim Felix refused to accept the resignation, telling her to take some time off, to get away. As Ferdi now reminded her, it hadn't helped. In two months she was back. The Job had become more important than ever.

"It would be different this time," she assured Ferdi and tried to convince herself. "Back then when I tried to break away I had nothing else, no other interest. This time I'd have Randall and a completely different life."

Arenas nodded. "It certainly would be a different life."

They were interrupted by a tap at the door. Art Potts, Captain Jacoby's whip, looked in.

"We just got a call from the One-Nine for backup. A man in army uniform is strafing the yard of Julia Richman High with a semi-automatic."

Because it was both a Saturday and a special holiday, the duty hours had been shifted to cover the heavy crowd activity anticipated for later that evening, so both precincts responded to the 911 call with all available personnel. Norah rode with Ferdi. Sirens shrieking, they cut through the park at top speed, came out at Seventy-second Street and Fifth Avenue and headed straight over to Second Avenue. Though they ignored the lights and twisted in and out of traffic, they were not quick enough.

Chapter _____
_____ TWO

Police cars from every direction converged on the scene, circling the playground in the hope of spotting the perpetrator and cutting off his escape. They were too late. He was gone. Everyone was gone. The playground was empty.

The cars, arriving within seconds of each other, came to a halt and cut engines. Norah Mulcahaney was the first to get out; slamming the door shut behind her, she shattered the silence. After her, one by one, the other doors were opened and closed as the men and women in blue and the plainclothes officers moved forward.

Norah had hoped that few people would have been present that morning, but she'd forgotten about the monthly flea market. Hand-lettered banners proclaiming the event, balloons tethered along the perimeter, and the colored umbrellas of the food vendors provided a tragic contrast to the overturned stands. Scattered wares—clothing, jewelry, pots and pans, and broken china—told the story of terror. Seller and buyer had run for their lives. Since she lived only a few blocks over, Norah knew the area well, but she looked around as though for the first time.

The schoolyard was directly behind the brick building and consisted of basketball, baseball, and handball courts. Another area was sectioned off for the little ones, with monkey bars, swings, and a sandbox for the very youngest. At the border facing First Avenue, a row of trees already in full leaf shaded benches for senior citizens. The entire complex was bordered on the north by the First Alliance Church, across the street on the east by the Sloan-Kettering Cancer Center, and on the south by a branch of the New York Public Library and a row of mid-Victorian-style apartment houses.

Where were all the people?

Gun in hand, with Ferdi beside her, Norah walked slowly to the center of the yard, looking up at what seemed to be blank windows. The perpetrator could be lurking behind any one of them or on a rooftop. He could have set this up as an ambush, to draw together a force of police and open fire. The original shooting could have been a ruse. 911 had reported the perp was armed with a semi-automatic weapon, therefore he would be able to get most of them before anyone could locate where the fire was coming from. Norah's heart beat hard and fast; her senses were alert to receive any signal. It was the same with every man and woman there. It was what made it possible for them to do what had to be done, face what they had to face. Later, the reaction would set in and it was the reaction that ruined a lot of good cops. But Norah wasn't thinking about that. She had stopped thinking when she spotted the baby carriage just to the side of a concrete planter, near the entrance to the nursery area at Sixty-eighth, and the woman lying on the pavement a few feet away from it.

"Over here!" Norah shouted and waved. "Over here!"

She broke into a run, stopping just short of the woman and the carriage. The bullet marks formed a line across the woman's back. Like everybody else she'd been trying to get away, but the baby in the carriage had been an encumbrance. After a moment to steel herself, Norah walked past the woman to the carriage and looked inside.

The infant appeared to be sleeping. Norah touched his cheek—rosy, still warm, but she could detect no breathing. The bullet tracks across the pretty blue-and-white embroidered blanket were evidence that she wouldn't find a pulse either. Yet she didn't see blood. The baby's blood must have seeped down into the mattress, she thought, but how much blood could there be in that tiny body? At least, it was over quickly; she prayed to God that the baby had experienced neither fear nor pain. Then she went back and knelt beside the still form of the woman. Norah motioned for Ferdi, but he didn't respond right away.

"Ferdi," she called. "What's the matter? Are you all right?"

He shook himself, then joined her and they gently turned the victim over.

So young! Norah thought. She couldn't be more than sixteen, probably less although she'd tried to look older. Her dark hair was crimped into tight corkscrew curls. Her makeup was heavy, but it didn't hide the adolescent acne. She wore an elegant white, Chanel-style pants suit trimmed with gold braid, much too sophisticated for her. Front and back it was soaked with blood. Her dark eyes were wide open and filled with terror. She had known there was no hope, Norah thought, known it at the first burst of gunfire and at the first hit. She had tried to save the baby by shoving the perambulator one way and herself turning to run in the opposite direction toward the school building.

Carefully, Norah placed her fingertips just under the side of the jaw, feeling for the carotid artery as she had done with the baby. No response. They were both dead.

Together, she and Ferdi turned the girl back to her original position. "Make the notifications," she told Ferdi as they both got up. "Make sure somebody from the ME's office is on the way. I mean, right now."

"Yes, Lieutenant." As usual when they were working, Ferdi was formal. He was also on this occasion withdrawn.

Ferdi was the father of twin girls and recently Concepción had given birth to a third child, a son, Ricardo. To be able to spend more time with his family, Ferdi had moved them from Forest Hills into the city. Like Norah, they lived not far from here. In fact, she had helped them find the apartment. "Do you know this girl? Have you seen her in the neighborhood?"

"No, but the size of the carriage . . . You notice the size, Lieutenant?"

"It's large."

"It's for two. It's like the one we had for the twins. They've outgrown it, but sometimes the baby-sitter takes Ricardo out in it. Sometimes, she comes here."

"And you thought . . . I'm so sorry, Ferdi. Maybe you should go home. Why don't you?"

He swallowed. "No, I'm okay. I'll go make the notifications."

He wasn't okay, Norah thought, but it might be best for him to work it off. She nodded. "When you contact Ballistics, advise them we need an expert in semi-automatics."

Next Norah waved Wyler over.

"There had to be more than one complaint phoned in. Contact 911. Get the names and addresses of the callers." She pointed to the Public Library. "There'll be a phone in there."

Next, she summoned Detectives Neel and Ochs. "I want to talk to the witnesses. Obviously, the people who were here when the perp started shooting scattered and ran for cover. They'll be coming out soon. Make sure nobody gets away till we have their names and addresses. Danny, you take the north side. Take a look in the church."

"Right, Lieutenant."

Detective Second-Grade Daniel Neel came from three generations of cops. His grandfather had been a full Inspector, and he intended to go right up the ladder past his grandfather. He was a fine looking lad with dark curly hair, a good set of teeth, and a dimple at the left of his chin. Big, strong, he boxed for the police team in the middleweight division.

"Julius, you take the east side," Norah directed Ochs. "Start with the cancer clinic. Some people might have run in there."

Physically, Detective First-Grade Julius Ochs was Neel's direct opposite, but he had plenty of brains. As far as career goals went, he was aiming just as high.

"Yes, ma'am," Ochs replied and crossed the street.

Once more Norah looked around the deserted playground, desolate under the ominous clouds. Once more she studied the line of fire. It had cut through the two victims and after that the weapon had been pointed straight down into the pavement for a stretch and then abruptly the bullet marks appeared along the wall of the school, high, well above the average person's head. She made a note in her book, a habit ingrained in every rookie and never forgotten.

The sky darkened; a sulphuric yellow glow marked the edges of the storm area. Norah called to one of the uniforms for a tarpaulin from the trunk of his patrol car, then returned to the girl for another look.

She had good legs and small, pretty feet shod in high-heeled, expensive, lizard pumps. They were the real thing; Norah knew the difference between genuine reptile and machine-stamped imitations. She looked for the purse. It hadn't been under her when she and Ferdi turned her over, which probably meant she kept it in the baby carriage. Yes, tucked under the blanket at the baby's feet was the handbag, also lizard to match the shoes. Along with the suit, the whole outfit must have run well over a thousand dollars.

The purse contained a couple of letters addressed to Dolores Lopez, 319 East Sixty-ninth Street, and bearing the postmark of Mayagüez, P.R., a wallet with six hundred dollars in grimy, worn bills, and the usual assortment of cosmetics—lipstick, compact, mascara, eyelash curler, and so forth.

As she sorted through the dead girl's belongings, Norah became aware that people were emerging from the various buildings across the street from the playground, and forming a line along the edge of the sidewalk to maintain a safe distance. Most of them. One woman did break through.

"Cindy! Cindy! Where's my Cindy? Where's my little girl?"

Norah stepped in front of her to mask the body on the pavement and the baby carriage. "Was she supposed to be here?"

"Yes, yes. She said she was coming here. What happened? Where is she?"

"She came alone?"

"She's twelve years old." The woman was instantly on the defensive. "We live just across the street." She pointed to the building next to the library. "It's always been safe here. We've never had any trouble, not real trouble. Nothing . . . like this." She started to cry. "I was down in the basement doing laundry. I didn't hear . . . I didn't know . . . Oh, my God, where is my little girl?"

At that moment, the back door of the school was flung open and a crowd, mostly women and children, streamed out. Some were dazed and silent, some sobbing, all still in shock. One child shouted:

"Mommy! Mommy!"

Cindy ran into her mother's arms.

Norah let them go.

The job of talking to all these people, sifting through what they had experienced, through the emotion and the reality, seemed a staggering job, almost insurmountable. Then Norah took a deep breath, one step at a time, one interview at a time, she thought, exhaled and addressed the crowd.

"I'm Lieutenant Mulcahaney from the Twentieth Precinct. I know you're anxious to get home and I won't keep you any longer than absolutely necessary, but we need to know what happened here. Can anyone tell me?"

Eyes that had been fixed on Norah now turned away.

"You were lucky. You weren't even injured." She pointed to the two victims. "They're both dead."

A stocky, gray-haired woman wearing a gray warm-up suit with a white stripe at the shoulder stepped forward. "I sell hand-painted china. That's my stand over there." She pointed to an overturned display table, most of the fragile stock shattered on the pavement. "I was talking to a customer when I heard shots. I didn't realize they were shots. There's so much noise around here—construction, backfires—that I never thought . . . not till people started screaming and running. Then I saw a man wearing one of those jungle-type uniforms . . ."

"You mean an army uniform?"

"Yes. Green with blobs of brown. He had a cap pulled way down that hid his eyes and most of his face to his beard and he had this gun kind of tucked under his arm and he was spraying bullets, just spraying like he didn't care who he hit. Like he'd gone crazy." Her voice broke. Her eyes filled. "I'm sorry."

"No need, Mrs. . . . ?"

"Boyd. Philomena Boyd."

"You're being very helpful, Mrs. Boyd, and we really appreciate it. Did you happen to notice anything else about the shooter? Was he tall or short? You mentioned a beard; was the beard dark or light?"

Philomena Boyd stopped crying and concentrated instead. "I don't know about his height; he was kind of bent over, but his beard was dark and very bushy."

"All right. Thank you." Norah looked to the others. "Can anyone add to that?" She got no response. What could she expect when they had been fleeing for their lives? "But he was alone?" That brought scattered nods of assent. "And he didn't shoot from a car or from the street? He walked into the playground and stood . . . where?"

"There."

Several people responded by pointing to the first in a row of concrete planters. There were more nods of confirmation, some vigorous. So now Norah could move on.

She indicated the dead girl. "Her name is Dolores Lopez. She lives not far from here on East Sixty-ninth. Does anybody know her?" Instinctively and as a group, the people moved back. "Maybe you've seen her around the neighborhood?" She looked from person to person directly, but no one would meet her look. "Maybe you've noticed her with the baby, walking or sitting out here with the other mothers? Seen her in the market or the library?" No response. But somebody was holding back, Norah could sense it. She didn't press. Later, each person would be interviewed individually and at length. The entire neighborhood would be canvassed, statements checked and cross-checked by computer. Meantime, she signaled for a couple of officers.

"We'll need your name and address and then you can go on. . . ."

Another commotion had broken out at the police barricade. A woman shouted and struggled to shake off restraining hands. She was about twenty, dressed in a thigh-high, black leather skirt and black turtleneck sweater with plenty of gold jewelry. Her raven curls were disheveled, her olive skin blotchy, eyes red and swollen. She was at the edge of hysteria. At Norah's signal, she was released and came running out to where Dolores Lopez lay.

"*Madre de Dios,*" she murmured and crossed herself.

"Do you know her?" Norah asked softly. Getting no answer, she was about to kneel to turn the victim over, but it wasn't necessary.

"She's my sister. My little sister, Dolores."

"And the baby?"

"Her son."

"And what is your name, please?"

"Carmen. Carmen Herrera." She answered automatically, never looking at Norah, only at the body lying before her. Then, slowly, she walked on past the dead girl to the carriage. As Norah had done, she took a moment to brace herself and then looked inside. A soft sigh slipped from her. She reached down and gently, tenderly, placed her arms under the infant and lifted him out. She held him close to her bosom. "*Sh, niño, sh,*" she soothed and rocked him back and forth, crooning tunelessly.

Chapter THREE

Norah couldn't get the baby away from her. The woman appeared to have gone into a trance. She ignored Norah, her surroundings, the noise, the crowd. She continued to rock back and forth, crooning to the child as though they were alone in the nursery.

"Please, Ms. Herrera, there's nothing you can do for him. I'm sorry, but . . . it's too late."

Carmen Herrera either didn't hear or she refused to acknowledge she'd heard. "I'm taking him home."

"No. I'm sorry, you can't."

"He was my sister's child and now he's mine. I'm taking him home and you can't stop me."

Norah's heart went out to her.

"A doctor is on the way over. Why don't you let him take a look at the baby? All right, Ms. Herrera? He should be here any minute. Then we'll see. All right?"

"All right."

"Maybe you'd like to go inside and wait?" Norah indicated the school.

"No. We'll wait right here."

Norah didn't argue. A chair was found so that the woman with the dead infant in her arms could at least sit. And there they waited as the crowd grew larger. They might have been actors on a stage waiting for the audience to file into the theater, Norah thought.

Sirens signaled the arrival of the EMS come from nearby New York Hospital to help the survivors. The morgue wagon followed immediately after, then the Chief Medical Examiner, Phillip Worgan, got out of his car and made his way over. He was thirty-three, seemingly a stolid, unemotional person. In fact, he was a keen student of forensics and enthusiastic about his job. Having served a year as Acting Chief Medical Examiner, he had on the past January 31st been confirmed in tenure.

Emerging into the clearing, Worgan took in the situation, nodded to Norah, and knelt beside the victim. His examination, though brief, was far from perfunctory. When he was through, he signaled the attendants to bring the gurney. Then he went over to the woman cradling the infant.

"The sister," Norah whispered to him. "Ms. Herrera? Here's the doctor."

Carmen Herrera had stopped crying, but she didn't respond, not till Worgan reached for the child. Gently, he pried the baby away and she let him. When she looked at her empty hands and saw they were bloody and that the front of her sweater was stained with blood, she cried out.

"No! No!" She reached to get the baby back.

Norah put her arms around the trembling woman. "He's gone, Ms. Herrera. It's no use."

"Give him to me."

"Dr. Worgan just wants to take a look at him."

"You're going to take him away and cut him up. I won't allow it."

"You'll have him back in no time," Norah promised. Worgan was sending negative signals, but Norah ignored them. "All right, Ms. Herrera?"

"Can I go with him in the ambulance?"

This time Norah did consult Worgan. He frowned. He had already interrupted his schedule to respond to Norah Mulcahaney's urgent call for his presence, now he'd have to disrupt it further and give priority to at least one of the autopsies. Bad enough, but to have a civilian waiting . . .

"I'll come with her. I'll stay with her till you're done. Okay, Phil?"

"If you have nothing better to do."

"As a matter of fact, I don't."

Their eyes met and held. "Deal," he said and took the baby to the van himself before starting back to his own car. "See you downtown."

Reporters shouted questions, but Worgan ignored them. Flashbulbs went off in his face. He put up a hand to shield his eyes, but didn't bother to protest. They must be desperate for a story to want his picture, he thought.

Norah knew she was next and that she wouldn't get away so easily. She'd always enjoyed a good relationship with the media. Her most recent case, the Valente murder, had drawn public attention to her and she'd been invited to appear on Randall Tye's *People in the News* television show. At first, she'd been nervous in front of the camera, but Tye was an expert at drawing out his guests and he succeeded in making Norah angry enough to speak what was on her mind. The network switchboard lit up, and she found herself an instant celebrity. She was not only investigating the murder of a top *Mafioso,* but representing the NYPD. She was, in fact, doing a PR job. She became skillful in dealing with reporters, interviewers, and most particularly with the "working stiffs," some of whom were here now shouting and waving to get her attention.

She had no intention of ignoring them, but first she reminded Ochs and Neel to make sure nobody left without giving his name and address. "If anybody's willing to make a statement, escort them to the squad. Don't give them a chance to change their minds."

After both gurneys had been lifted into the van and secured, Norah walked over to the police barrier. Her raised hands brought, if not silence, at least a reduction of noise from the press and television contingent.

"I can't tell you anything because I don't know anything." The announcement was met by a ripple of disbelieving laughter. "I'm going to ride down to the morgue with the victims."

That was unusual and was greeted with a low buzz. As Carmen Herrera was helped into the back, somebody, one of the CBS people, yelled.

"Who is she? Who's the woman?" Flashbulbs punctuated the question.

"She's the victim's sister," Norah replied. "Give her a break, will you?"

With that, she, too, climbed in. Sirens wailing, the van turned the corner at Second Avenue and headed downtown.

Carmen Herrera was silent on the ride to Thirtieth Street and the Office of the Medical Examiner of the City of New York. Norah made no attempt to draw her out; it was not the time. Upon arrival, they would of necessity be separated from the victims and put in a waiting room and then she might turn to Norah of her own accord. And so she did.

"The baby, Charlito . . ." Tears filled Carmen's eyes. "The baby is illegitimate. My little sister got into trouble. My family in Puerto Rico, they do not take such a thing lightly. I went down there to be with her and as soon as she gave birth and could travel I brought her and the baby back with me. Here, nobody cares about such things.

"I was so happy to have them here. Dolores and I, we were always very close. As for the baby, I wanted a baby. Juan and I, my husband and I, we've been trying, but we haven't had any luck. So Charlito was like my very own."

Norah and Joe had wanted a child and had not been able to have one. Then they'd adopted and had had to give up that child. She could understand Carmen's pain.

"How long was Dolores with you?"

"About five months."

"And she lived with you and your husband in your apartment?"

"Yes."

"Did she make any friends?"

"No."

"Did she date?"

"No. She wasn't interested. She was very bitter."

"The baby's father? He just abandoned her?"

"That's right. My father was very angry. He would have forced them to marry, but Dolores wouldn't say who it was."

No motive there, Norah thought. "Who might want to kill your sister? Have you any idea?"

Carmen Herrera shook her head. "It was an accident, wasn't it? The man who shot them—he was crazy, wasn't he?"

So far everything indicated she was right, that this was one more of the random killings committed by an unbalanced person seeking release of the rage within. According to the reports of the witnesses interviewed so far, the shooter had sprayed the bullets in every direction.

Norah sought to calm Mrs. Herrera. "What part of Puerto Rico do you come from?"

"Mayagüez," she replied automatically. "Why would anybody want to hurt Dolores and the baby? What will I tell my parents? They'll blame me for letting it happen."

"How long have you been living in New York?"

"About three years. My husband came up first and then he sent for me."

"He must be doing well in order to bring up your sister and her child."

"He has a gas station on York Avenue."

"Would you like me to call him?"

Carmen Herrera shook her head and looked toward the door.

The man who stood poised there was strikingly good-looking, with dusky skin, nobly chiseled features, high brow, and full red lips, the lower dipping sensuously at the center. His black hair swept back in waves just brushing at the chin line. He wore a single gold earring with a small diamond in it. There was only one thing to spoil the effect: he was short, not more than five-six. Not a midget by any means, but Norah could tell by the way he carried himself, by the stance he took immediately upon entering, that it bothered him and that everything he did was based on his stature, or lack of it. He wore a bombardier-style jacket of softest fawn leather which emphasized massive shoulders and well-developed pectoral muscles; his slacks were wool of a slightly darker shade, custom-made.

He took a couple of steps into the room, held out his arms, and let his wife come to him.

"Los mataron," she wailed, resting her head against his chest. *Por qué? Por qué los mataron?"*

"Cálmate, querida. Cálmate." He kissed her cheek lightly. "Who are you?" he asked Norah.

"Lieutenant Mulcahaney, Homicide."

"What's my wife doing in this place? Why did you bring her here?"

"It was her idea. She insisted. She wanted to be close to her sister and the baby."

"And you came with her to keep her company, is that it? You dropped everything to stay with her because you felt sorry for her, is that right, Lieutenant? Or was it to take advantage of her emotional state? To ask questions and get answers you might not get otherwise."

"Such as?"

"Whatever suits your purpose."

"All I want is to find out who killed your sister-in-law and her child."

"Then go and do it. You had no right to bring my wife here and to subject her to interrogation. She hasn't been well since her last miscarriage. She loved that little baby. He meant the world to her. Now, with the double tragedy . . . God knows what damage you've caused."

Norah met his anger straight on. "It was not my intention to do anything but offer comfort."

"That's not your job."

Supported by the current interpretation of civil rights, he had chosen to attack. He had backed Norah into a corner, and she, filled with compassion for his wife's grief, had allowed him to do it. There was nothing now but to apologize. "I'm sorry."

His glare now held a gleam of satisfaction. "You should be." He took off his jacket and put it about his wife's shoulders. "Come on, *querida,* I'm taking you home."

"*Y el niño?*"

"*Está con Dios.*" He picked up his sister-in-law's handbag and looked around. "Is this everything?" he asked Norah.

"Everything she had with her."

"What happened to the baby carriage?"

"That's gone to the lab for examination. After they're through, it will be sent to the property clerk's office. Unless it's needed as evidence, you can claim it there."

Herrera shrugged. "I guess we won't be needing it." Linking arms with his wife, he led her out without a backward glance.

Before leaving the crime scene, Norah had instructed Ferdi and the rest of her people to keep at the canvass till the end of the shift. Whatever section had not been covered should be passed along to the men coming on duty. So when she left the morgue, Norah returned to get the report of the first team. The descriptions of the shooter varied. Some said he was tall, some short; to some he appeared heavy, to others slim. That was not unusual; in moments of stress, impressions were subjective, could, in fact, be based on the witness's past experience. However, all witnesses interviewed so far agreed that he wore army uniform with a soft cap pulled well down, hiding his hair and shadowing his eyes, and that a heavy, dark beard obscured the lower half of his face. He had appeared out of nowhere and opened fire without warning. Naturally, everybody had scrambled for cover. They crouched behind cars and garbage cans, behind display tables. They kept their heads down: Till they were sure he was gone.

However, it turned out he was not a total stranger. He had been observed around the neighborhood in uniform but without the gun, of course. He had shown up only recently and nobody knew where he lived. It was assumed he lived nearby but that didn't have to be the case. Nobody talked to him, in fact, most of those who had observed him took care to avoid him. The ordinary citizen had long since learned to steer clear of the unfortunate and the disturbed. He was just one more weirdo.

Simon Wyler brought in the only lead.

"A couple of boys claim he sometimes spent the night in the old firehouse on Sixty-seventh right across from the Russian Mission." That building along with the original 19th Precinct Station House had been completely gutted and under reconstruction for nearly four years and was still nowhere near finished. It barely offered protection from the elements.

"The kids put together a shack they use for a clubhouse. They smoke a little pot and sometimes they pick up stuff the construction crew leaves behind—tools, copper piping, anything they can sell. One night they spotted this guy at the back. He'd made a shelter out of canvas draped over a couple of shopping carts and was sleeping inside. They woke him, intending to have some fun and run him out, but he grabbed a two-by-four and sent them running instead. They didn't mention it to anybody, but they didn't go back either."

"Okay," Norah told Wyler. "You and Neel stake out the site." That would mean overtime, but in view of the heavy assignment of personnel to cover the anniversary festivities, she had no choice. "Tedesco and Aldrege will relieve you." She paused. The man the boys had observed could have been a vagrant or the killer. If the latter and he was still armed, and no reason to think otherwise, would two men be enough?

"I'll get you backup," she promised.

Alone in her office, Norah slumped at her desk. It was over nine hours since the call requesting assistance had come in. When the case was established as a homicide, it fell in the jurisdiction of the Fourth Zone. Having notified the downtown brass, Norah and her squad went into action, amassing a great deal of information to be sorted out and evaluated. That was Norah's job, but she could do it just as well at home in pajamas and slippers and with her feet up.

A series of flashes lit the darkness outside and were followed by sharp detonations. Fireworks, Norah thought, and then when the wind whipped heavy sheets of rain against the window, she realized this was the storm that had been threatening all day. The decision had been made for her; she certainly wasn't going out in this. She put on her reading glasses and settled to work.

After a while, she had no idea how long, she sensed someone was at the door.

"Yes?"

The door opened. "Remember me?"

Randall Tye stood on the threshold.

"Randall!" Norah bit her lip. "I forgot. I'm so sorry. I forgot all about the party."

"There was no party. When I heard, I called it off."

She shouldn't have been surprised, either at the extent of his information nor his sensitivity.

"I'm anchoring a special tomorrow night on the schoolyard shootings. I didn't talk to any of your people, I got the facts from my own sources. I'm not trying to scoop you or the department. Okay?"

"It's okay as long as you don't broadcast something that might compromise the investigation."

"I'd never do that."

"You're not in a position to judge."

"You want to censor the content of the show?"

"Not censor." This was what Norah had been fearing would happen. By mutual agreement, they had scrupulously avoided intruding into the other's territory. "Not censor, I just want to check what you intend to make public."

"Will you give me what you've got? Shall we compare notes?"

"I can't do that. You know I can't."

"You want me to trust you. Then you'll have to trust me."

"I don't question your good intention, but you might inadvertently let something slip."

"Now you're insulting both my judgment and my capability," Randall Tye retorted. "I didn't have to come over here and advise you in advance about the show. I could just have gone on the air and let you find out along with everybody else."

"Yes, you could."

"So let's pretend I haven't said anything and I'll take you home. Unless you want to stop for a hamburger on the way?"

Norah took a deep breath. "I could use a hamburger. Even two. In fact, I could use a night out. Soon."

His amber eyes lit up. "You've got it. Tomorrow, right after the show."

Norah frowned. If she didn't have a commitment, then he did. "I had in mind something ordinary—no celebrities, no network big shots, just the two of us. Dinner and a movie maybe. But you won't be able to shake loose and it'll be too late, anyway."

"I'll shake loose and it won't be too late. We'll rent a movie and send out for a pizza. How's that?"

Norah grinned. "I love it."

Randall took her hands in his. "What we really need is to get away for a few days. Completely. Like the time we went to New Paltz."

Norah had had some vacation coming, and, whereas she usually squandered it doing meaningless chores around the house, Randall had insisted that even four days could be made to count. Clearing his own schedule, no easy task, he appointed himself travel agent and booked rooms in an old, Gothic-style hotel nestled above Lake Mohonk in the Hudson Valley. Though not far from New York, it was an area natural, unspoiled, unpolluted.

For the first time in their relationship, Norah and Randall were on neutral ground. Instead of competing, they shared the beauty around them. They climbed the mountain trails to look down on the pristine waters of the lake and see the reflection of trees and sky. They rode horseback. Neither was expert, so they could laugh at each other's ineptitudes. Later, they groaned together over their aches and pains. Never before had Norah sat still to watch a sunset. She shared four with Randall, not moving till the moment when the last wisp of rose and crimson had faded into night. After dinner they played chess, although neither was very good at that, either. They retired early so they could get up at sunrise and go bird-watching. There had been no sex. Randall had put no moves on her. She'd wondered many times since how she would have responded.

"What do you say, sweetheart? Want to go back?" Randall asked.

Norah's face glowed. "I can't think of anything I'd like better."

Chapter
FOUR

They dressed in silence—Judith Barthelmess at the vanity, applying her makeup, Representative William Barthelmess in the bathroom of the luxurious Plaza Hotel suite, shaving.

It wasn't going well and they both knew it, but neither would admit it to the other. Each new round of fund-raisers rekindled hope, only to have it snuffed out again. The campaign was deeply in debt. Credit was no longer available from newspapers, the television stations, airlines: they wanted cash in advance, and that was the first ominous portent of defeat. They were operating on a week-to-week basis and unless contributions started coming in, and in substantial amounts, it would soon be down to day-to-day. Politics had become, in fact had been for a considerable time, a rich man's game. Idealism, hard work, enthusiastic volunteers didn't count for much. It cost money to throw your hat in the ring and keep it there to the primaries, and plenty more if you managed to get your name on the ballot for November. If you didn't have a private fortune, you had to go out and raise money. Beg for it.

I'm not a good beggar, Will Barthelmess thought as he rinsed out the razor.

He studied his image in the mirror of the elegant bathroom with its gold-plated fixtures. They couldn't afford all this luxury, he thought. They should have stayed with his parents in Queens. That would have made points with the middle class and the blue collars, but, as Judith had pointed out, they weren't in New York to woo them. That would come later, maybe. They were here on the two-hundredth anniversary of the inauguration of the first president, ostensibly to attend the festivities. Tonight there was the concert in the park and tomorrow the official reenactment of the inauguration on the steps of Federal Hall. But the real purpose of the trip was to raise money so that the Representative could become the Senator. With that goal in view, Will and Judith Barthelmess would be attending three private, prestigious affairs: two cocktail receptions, the first at the home of Sophie Callendar, widow of the legendary Pat Callendar, four-term governor of the state of New York, the other hosted by Mr. and Mrs. Edward Lavansky, representing old money and influence. These two would be direct and express appeals to fill the Barthelmess campaign coffers. The main event, however, would be the dinner given in honor not of the candidate but of the state's party chairman, Ralph Dreeben. Though retiring, Dreeben made it plain he was not abdicating. He intended to use his power, to remain an *éminence grise*. Being invited to his testimonial dinner, therefore, was an indication of the chairman's support. Direct requests for contributions from others present would come later.

To get money you had to look like you didn't need it, Judith said, and as usual Judith was right—about the suite and about everything else. She was his greatest asset, after his looks, naturally. Will studied himself in the bathroom mirror and splashed on the after-shave.

On the down side of forty, he had aged well so far. The pouches under his hazel eyes, the lines at his mouth, suggested maturity of mind and hard work in public service. His youth showed in the thickness of his brown hair and the total absence of gray. His brow was high, his jaw strong. Women were attracted to him; men didn't resent him. Yet, it wasn't in him to ask for money. Judith was the one who could promote, publicize, and charm potential supporters into opening their checkbooks.

The phone rang. Though there was an extension right there beside the tub, Barthelmess made no move to pick it up. It was established practice that the candidate never answered the telephone; he might be trapped into talking to someone he wished to avoid, forced to make an inconvenient commitment, or to turn one down, even to be cornered by a member of the media! At campaign headquarters, a secretary would answer. At home, the maid. On the campaign trail, Judith.

The ringing broke off, so he knew she was on the line in the bedroom. He heard her say, "Yes?" then he stopped listening. Probably it concerned some detail about tonight's activities. He wasn't really interested.

"Hello, Ralph."

Judith Barthelmess forced pleasure and cordiality into her voice, forced, not because she didn't like Ralph Dreeben as a person or appreciate his position of power in the party, but because she was feeling very discouraged.

"How are you, Judith?" the chairman asked.

"Fine," she lied. "Got a little virus that's dragging me down, but otherwise I'm okay. What's happening?"

"I've got big news. Nicolson is withdrawing from the race."

"No!" Lorne Nicolson was the incumbent senator; he had held the seat for twelve years and had been regarded as close to invincible. Lately he'd made a few errors, misspoken himself, blundered on facts, but nothing his reputation couldn't overcome. "Why?" Judith asked cautiously.

"He says because his wife is sick."

"I didn't know. I'm sorry." It was a standard excuse for a candidate who could taste defeat, who had lost his stomach for the fight. Nicolson didn't fall into that category. Maybe he was looking ahead and decided to cash in his assets while their value was still high. He could even be telling the truth.

There was a pause filled with their unspoken thoughts.

"Has he indicated whom he'll support?" Judith Barthelmess asked.

"We're negotiating."

"Ah . . ." That was it then, Judith thought. What they were talking about here was more than votes. With the incumbent's retirement from the field there would be a grab for Nicolson's campaign staff, media experts, money men. If Nicolson threw his support their way, these benefits would go with it and it would be a tremendous coup. If he endorsed someone else, it could be disastrous. And Nicolson knew the power he wielded and was hardly likely to step down without making an endorsement.

"What does he want?" Judith asked.

"We'll have to see."

"When will he announce?"

"After our meeting."

Which meant Dreeben had the situation well in control. "Anything I can do?"

"I'll let you know."

That was their deal and had been from the start.

After she hung up, Judith Barthelmess stared into the vanity mirror.

Everyone called her and Will an attractive couple, but it was Will who had the looks; she had to work at holding her end up. In politics, it wasn't a bad thing for the woman to be less than glamorous, unless she was the candidate herself and that was another story and carried different rules. Judith's face was long and narrow. Her eyes were pale, an indeterminate color between blue and gray. Her auburn hair was long and silky and she kept it well-brushed and coiled into a severe French knot. Judith Barthelmess had long since accepted that she couldn't be pretty, but she would be stylish. Not too stylish, not so much that she would draw attention away from Will, but enough so that his attention wouldn't stray from her. She had loved him since high school. He had been head of the debating society, president of the student council. He had shied from contact sports, but he was on the tennis and swimming teams. Judith admired him as did all the girls, and being herself an exceptional student, she was able to follow him to the college of his choice, where his record continued to be outstanding and hers lagged only slightly. They were married on graduation and went on to law school.

They passed their bar exams at the same time. Will got a job in the DA's office, more concerned with how it would look on his résumé when he ran for office than with the money it brought in. Judith took on the responsibility of making ends meet by moving into real estate, where she was very successful. They put off having children. Now, Judith thought feeling the flush of hope in her cheeks, the moment could be at hand. If Ralph Dreeben got Nicolson to swing his support to them . . .

Will's first campaign had been a disaster. He had been running for a seat in the state assembly, a modest aim. He was filled with idealism, crusading zeal to solve the problems of the inner city without ignoring the rural areas or the industrial complex. He never got his message to the voters in that first attempt, never had the chance to be judged because he had to drop out for lack of funds.

That was a lesson neither he nor Judith ever forgot: you can't compete, never mind win or lose, without money.

"Will?" Judith called and rose, gathering the silky negligee around her and waiting till he came out of the bathroom into the bedroom. "Guess what? Nicolson is going to withdraw."

"No!" Barthelmess exclaimed. "Has he announced?"

"Not yet."

"Has he indicated to whom he'll swing his support?"

"Dreeben's meeting with him."

"Wow!" He grinned.

Maybe she shouldn't have mentioned it till it was set, Judith thought. Maybe she shouldn't have got his hopes up, but he'd been so depressed lately. He needed encouragement, and Ralph was not one to lose out on a deal he wanted.

"Wow, indeed."

Letting the silken gauze of the wrap fall open, she moved close, reached up and put her arms around his neck, her nipples hardening against his bare chest.

It was a long time since they'd had sex, Will thought. Too long. He could feel his desire growing. Cupping her breasts in his hands, he bent down to nuzzle them.

She groaned with pleasure, then abruptly pulled back.

"We're late already, sweetheart."

Ralph Dreeben hung up satisfied with the result of the telephone conversation. Judith Barthelmess was strong, as ambitious as her husband and more of a pragmatist. A commitment from her was as good as from Barthelmess himself. Better. She would not forget and she would see to it that Will did not renege.

Reluctantly, Ralph Dreeben had decided to retire. The opposition headed by Hal Rutenberg had been chipping away at him since the last election, which Dreeben had won by a hair, or Rutenberg had lost by a sigh, depending from which side you viewed it. Dreeben's support came principally from the Hispanic community. He was like a godfather to the poor who came seeking his help. He always found a way; he never turned a suppliant down. In return, he could count on their vote. He could deliver them as a solid block, which very often represented the balance of power in the political back rooms. But the size of his constituency was dwindling. New leaders representing other ethnical interests challenged him and he was realist enough to know that he could not survive. Quit while you're ahead had always been his motto. Maybe with Charlotte still alive, he might have withdrawn more gracefully, but his wife of twenty-four years had died of cancer in September. That was nearly eight months ago, yet in the lonely late hours a shadow on the wall would make him catch his breath in the sudden hope that she was there, that somehow her death and the funeral were a terrible nightmare. His heart would jump. On the street, a brief glimpse of someone like her would make the loss raw again.

The chairman was sixty-eight, heavyset, hair snow-white, complexion ruddy, suggesting good health but actually an indication of high blood pressure and that he was drinking too much. There were no children. Dreeben was not interested in women. In the years of his marriage he had never been unfaithful. Now that he was alone, he had nothing but the schemes and intrigues of politics to sustain him. He was accustomed to working behind the scenes, to getting what he wanted through the actions of others. So like the prudent steward in the Bible, Ralph Dreeben was making friends for himself now while he had something to give in order to be able to call in his markers later. Influence with a U.S. Senator could be a big card.

But he didn't want to withdraw from the public eye completely. It occurred to him that the murder of that woman and baby in the school-yard he'd heard about on the six o'clock news might serve. In the old days, he would have been informed of the shooting almost as soon as it had happened. He would have known the first name of every cop and every detective, and they would have known him and welcomed his presence on the scene. But those days were gone. Nevertheless, he still had sources, good sources, and after only a couple of calls he got the information he wanted.

As far as was known then, the killing was the work of a solitary gunman. A man in uniform, carrying a semi-automatic, had appeared in the midst of the flea-market crowd consisting largely of women and children and opened fire without apparent instigation. It seemed to be the act of an unbalanced person spewing out his despair. God only knew why. It was happening too often, almost losing the power to shock. But this murder of mother and baby would certainly rouse the public, he thought. There was bound to be an outcry, and he deter-mined to put himself at the head of it.

His first move was to contact Chief of Detectives Luis Deland.

After expressing shock and outrage, he asked if in addition to the two fatalities there had been other injuries.

"Thank God, no," Deland replied.

"That's a miracle, don't you think?" Dreeben asked.

The C of D offered no comment.

"The people who escaped must be in shock."

"They are," Deland agreed readily. "We're asking those who were in the vicinity but didn't come under fire—pedestrians, persons in the buildings overlooking the schoolyard—anyone who observed the event, to step forward. So far nobody has."

That was his opening and Dreeben seized it. "I was thinking—that's my old district, or it was before I moved to Queens, and the people still have confidence in me. If I made a direct appeal, someone might respond."

"How do you mean, a direct appeal?"

"Go on the air. Make a tape that could be shown on the news and then at intervals. In the nature of a public announcement. What do you think?"

Ralph Dreeben had served as an elected official for one term only in the state assembly in Albany, but as party boss he had dispensed jobs and contracts and every variety of patronage for many years. He was idolized and his support was greater now than it had ever been.

Deland knew it. He knew the politician's offer was self-serving. The Chief had been sitting in the same chair for many years; he had an instinct for assessing a case. Murder in the streets had become ordinary; *God help us all,* he thought, chewing on an unlit cigar which, since a second heart attack four months ago, was the only taste of tobacco he allowed himself. Up to now open gunfire had been limited to the outskirts of the city—Howard Beach, Bensonhurst, the Rockaways. Now the inevitable had happened, innocent blood had been spilled in the heart of Manhattan.

"I appreciate the cooperation, Mr. Dreeben. I'll have Chief Felix set it up and get back to you."

Chapter

FIVE

Norah's phone rang at 5:38 the next morning. Her sleep had been shallow, her senses just below the level of consciousness, so that she woke instantly and was completely alert. She expected the call to be from either Tedesco or Aldrege reporting that the suspect had walked into the gutted firehouse and they had him in custody. She had thrown back the covers and swung her legs over the side of the bed ready to bounce to her feet when the caller, whose voice she didn't recognize, identified himself as Sergeant Walsh from the office of the C of D and ordered her to report to Chief Deland *forthwith*. It was not the first time Norah had been summoned by the Chief of Detectives, so she wasn't nervous. The murder of mother and child in the schoolyard had sent shock waves through the public, and rocked the department. In the midst of the bicentennial festivities Chief Deland was calling a council of war; the hour indicated both the urgency and the intention to keep the meeting small to avoid attracting attention. Norah wondered who else would be there.

Counting Deland himself, it turned out to be a total of four. Bureau Chief James Felix and Captain Emmanuel Jacoby, commander of the Two-Oh and Norah's boss, and Norah.

Luis Deland had held the post of Chief of Detectives under a series of Police Commissioners and through at least two changes of administration in City Hall. He was rightly perceived as being a skilled, honest, and dedicated cop and essential to the running of the detective division which consisted of approximately three thousand men and women, a great many of whom he knew by name. A tall, shambling man, he looked as though he didn't eat regularly, and the ever present, puffy bags under his eyes suggested he didn't get much sleep. Both were true. Neither food nor sleep had a high priority on Deland's schedule. For them he substituted a cheap brand of cigars. Norah couldn't recall ever having seen the chief without a stogie in his mouth, although now they remained unlit.

James Felix, a three-star chief, was Deland's executive officer. He was as hardworking and as smart as his boss; Deland would have tolerated no less. Felix was fifty-four and, with his penetrating green eyes and lean, lantern-jawed face, could have passed for mid-forties except that his roan-colored hair had gone completely white. He had over thirty years on the force and everybody expected he would get his fourth star and would be the next Chief of Detectives when, if ever, Deland stepped down. Norah was glad Felix was there. He had been Joe's close friend first and then hers. Many considered Felix to be her "rabbi," her sponsor, the person who promoted her career, who got her the good assignments and covered her rear in case of a foul-up. Certainly, he'd kept his eyes on her, been there to advise her, but he had never favored her over another, nor pushed her into an assignment for which she was not qualified.

Emmanuel Jacoby, although he was not the kind of officer to attract the attention of the brass by spectacular deed or brilliant investigation, was a strong administrator. He had reached his rank of Captain, the very top of the civil service promotion ladder, by dint of hard work, study, and high grades on exams. To go farther, even one step up to Deputy Inspector, required appointment. Responsibility for crowd control at the scene of the flea-market shooting would normally have devolved on either Midtown North or South, but both had been tied up with the anniversary festivities, so it had fallen on Manny Jacoby to take charge. It had been an opportunity to show what he could do in deployment of a large force.

Deland didn't waste any time. "The way the PC sees it, we've got two possibilities here. One, we're dealing with a repeater, and the perp is the same one who appeared dressed in army uniform and strafed the schoolyard in Brooklyn last month, killing five Amerasian kids. If that was once and this is twice, there'll be a third time. We can't allow it." He looked around. "Any ideas?"

Norah spoke up. "In the first case, I believe the perp only appeared to be shooting at random. He selected a school that had a large number of Amerasian students and chose to shoot into a group of them at the lunch break. I believe that when apprehended it will turn out he is in fact a veteran and his motive is linked to his war experiences." She paused for a moment, and Deland nodded for her to continue. "In this instance I was able to observe the line of fire. It went either directly down into the pavement or else well up above what would be the average person's head; except for the shots fired at the mother and the baby. They appear to have been specific targets."

"For what motive?" Deland asked.

"I don't know, sir. Yesterday's canvass turned up a couple of kids who noticed a homeless man answering the shooter's description wandering around the neighborhood during the past weeks. Sometimes, he sacked down in the old Sixty-seventh Street firehouse. We staked it out last night, but apparently he didn't show."

"If the kids noticed him, somebody else must have, too," Deland commented. "Continue the canvass and then go back over your tracks. Maybe you missed something." He turned to Felix. "She'll need more people."

"Right."

"We've got to get results fast. Whether it's the same perpetrator or a different one, we can't have women and children killed on the streets." Deland spoke in a flat, matter-of-fact manner, but everyone in the room sensed and shared the passion beneath.

"So, Lieutenant," Deland went on, "get the best description you can of this homeless man and have an Identikit portrait made. We'll cover the city with copies. Assemblyman Ralph Dreeben has offered to go on the air to appeal for information. You never know, it might work. We've got to try everything. We've got to take some action if only to show the public."

A light tap at the door interrupted. Sergeant Walsh looked in. "Excuse me, Chief. There's an urgent call for Lieutenant Mulcahaney. It's the lab, Lieutenant."

Norah flushed. "Tell them I'll call back."

"No, no," Deland countered. "Transfer the call in here, Sergeant."

Walsh left. They waited. After what seemed to Norah an interminable time, one of the phones on the chief's desk buzzed and, at his nod, she picked it up.

"Lieutenant Mulcahaney."

Though Deland occupied himself with selecting a fresh cigar, and Jim Felix rearranged papers in the file he held in his lap, and Manny

Jacoby fidgeted, Norah was nevertheless aware that she was being monitored by the top brass. What she heard, though, made her forget it.

"Are you sure? Are you sure it's not in some storeroom or closet?" she asked. "Of course, you've looked everywhere. Of course," she placated. "I don't suppose you had a chance to do any kind of examination? Not even a cursory . . . Yes, I know you only got it last night. I was hoping, that's all. . . . Thanks for letting me know."

She hung up. "The carriage in which Baby Charlito was killed is missing. It was turned over to the lab and now it's gone. Disappeared. Nobody knows what happened to it."

The disappearance of the baby carriage strongly supported Norah's theory that the shooting was no random eruption of violence, nevertheless the group decided to proceed on two parallel lines of investigation: one, that the shooter was unbalanced, randomly spraying a hail of bullets into a crowd; the other, that he had known exactly what he was doing and that the victims were his specific targets—in other words, in police parlance, that the killing was a "mystery."

Chief Felix would head up the search for the man in uniform, organizing a massive canvass to cover the areas of both shootings. It would serve to compare the two incidents and to make sure nothing had slipped through the cracks the first time in either of the precincts involved. Again, equally important from the chief's view, it would reassure the public that everything possible was being done.

Actually, Norah wasn't sorry to be relieved of the canvass. It was largely a job of rounding up personnel, and she preferred a "hands on" approach. Norah worked best with a small team so that she could give full play to her instincts and be in personal contact with witnesses. Some considered that a limitation. They said that because of it, Norah Mulcahaney would never rise above her present rank. Norah was aware of the rumors but paid them little heed. She was already mentally selecting the personnel she would use for this particular assignment and couldn't wait to get started.

But first she needed to know why Juan Herrera, in the midst of his agitation over the interrogation of his wife, had concerned himself with the baby carriage. Then, of course, she needed to know what had happened to the baby carriage. Lastly, and this she owed directly to Ferdi for she hadn't and wouldn't have noticed it herself—why was a carriage for two being used when there was only one child?

Chapter
SIX

Norah assigned Neel and Ochs to trace the baby carriage. Wyler was to be liaison with Chief Felix's side of the investigation. By noon, she and Ferdi were on their way to talk to the Herreras at their home. Aside from the fact that they worked well together, she had chosen Ferdi because he spoke Spanish. It could come in handy when dealing with an Hispanic witness.

The Herreras lived one block up from the playground where the shooting had taken place. Yesterday's storm had passed leaving a day that was more like June than early May, yet both playground and park were deserted. No youngsters used the basketball courts; no mothers sat on the benches chatting companionably while their toddlers squealed over their games or climbed the monkey bars. The yellow plastic police crime-scene tape was the only tangible reminder of the tragedy.

The building in which the Herreras lived was built in the thirties, elaborately decorated with pediments and columns in neoclassic style. Unfortunately, fire escapes had been added and they spoiled the handsome façade. Norah and Ferdi took the small automatic elevator up to the top floor, the eleventh, and rang the doorbell of Apartment C. Herrera opened the door. He didn't move aside. He didn't say anything.

"May we come in?" Norah asked.

"What for?"

"To talk."

"We've already talked."

"I don't understand your antagonism, Mr. Herrera. Under the circumstances I would have expected cooperation."

He glared with the same arrogance he'd shown at their first meeting.

"Okay, Lieutenant, I'll cooperate, but not now. Now is not a good time. My wife is still very upset. When she feels better . . ."

"*Quién es? Quién está a la puerta?*"

Carmen Herrera appeared at her husband's shoulder. She was drawn, almost haggard.

"Lieutenant Mulcahaney, Mrs. Herrera. And this is Sergeant Arenas. May we come in?"

Juan Herrera shrugged with annoyance, but at his wife's nod stepped aside.

They entered a narrow passage that opened into a long, high-ceilinged room freshly plastered and painted stark white. The floors were random oak, highly polished, bare. The furniture was contemporary, oversized, overstuffed, California blond. An elaborate stereo, large-screen television and VCR system stood against the length of one wall. Through an open door, Norah could see a galley-style kitchen. Though it was small and so narrow one person could not pass another easily, it was equipped with the newest hi-tech appliances. Norah noted the trademarks—the best on the market. She was sure the other apartments in the old building were not similarly equipped. But she was most interested in the luggage stacked near the bedroom door, a matched set of Vuitton. First class again, she thought.

"Going somewhere?"

Carmen answered. "Home. I'm going home to bury my dead. I'm going to bury the two of them where they won't be lonely—with the family, in my country."

"When are you going?"

Carmen's eyes filled. "As soon as . . . as soon as Dolores and the baby are released. I'll travel on the same plane with them."

"You're going with your wife, Mr. Herrera?"

"No. Unfortunately, it's not possible for me to leave at this time. I have business to attend to."

"At the garage?"

"That's right."

"There's no one who could take care of it for you? Maybe you could close down for a day or so?"

"Carmen has a large family in Mayagüez. She will not be alone."

Except on the trip, Norah thought. She would be alone with her dead sister and the infant she had loved like her own. "When will you be back, Mrs. Herrera?"

"I don't know."

"She'll stay awhile." Realizing he had spoken too firmly, more in the tone of an order than information, Herrera put an arm around his wife. "She'll rest in the sun, get well again. Have you ever been to Mayagüez, Lieutenant?"

"Only San Juan."

"Mayagüez is what San Juan used to be like. It's the real Puerto Rico. Carmen will stay and rest. She'll come back rejuvenated."

Carmen shrugged him off. "I may not come back."

"Oh, you will. Of course, you will, *querida.*"

"Don't be so sure," she replied and started for the bedroom.

"Carmen!" he called after her. "Carmen, come back here," he called again, but she closed the door firmly behind her. "She doesn't mean it," he told Norah and Ferdi. "She's still very upset."

The front doorbell rang. Herrera admitted two men, one black and the other white, both in gray overalls with a patch of the St. Vincent de Paul Society on the shirt pocket.

"You got stuff you want to donate?" the black man asked; he was the older and in charge.

"This way."

Herrera led them down an inside hallway to a closed door. As he opened it and the men went through, Norah and Ferdi had a glimpse of cheery, yellow wallpaper figured with Disneyland characters—Mickey Mouse, the Seven Dwarfs, Cinderella, Donald Duck. There were large cartons, stacks of baby clothes on the grooming table, and heaps of stuffed toys.

"What goes?" the black man asked.

"All of it."

"Furniture, too? Nobody told us there was furniture. I don't know if it will all fit in the van. We'll take what we can and come . . ."

"I want it all to go now," Herrera said. "Now," he repeated, with a glance toward the door of the other bedroom, which remained closed. Digging into his pants pockets, he pulled out a wad of bills and unpeeled a couple. "Get this stuff out as fast as you can. Get rid of it."

The trucker looked at the money. "You're the boss." He motioned his buddy into the room.

"And the baby carriage?" Norah asked Herrera.

"You said the lab had it, and after they were through it would be turned over to the property clerk."

"I'm afraid it's disappeared," she confessed. "Somebody took it. Have you any idea who that could be?"

"Somebody who needs a baby carriage."

"We'll get it back. Don't worry."

"Hey, no sweat. It doesn't matter."

"You don't want it back? You wanted it yesterday."

"I wanted to know where it was," he corrected. "I wanted to make sure some well-meaning jackass didn't show up at our front door with the damn thing. You've seen my wife; can you imagine what that would have done to her?"

Norah decided not to challenge that, for now.

"One more thing then and we're through. Where were you Saturday at the time of the shooting?"

"Me? I was at the garage. My employees will vouch for that. So will the customers I served. I can go through my vouchers and give you a list, if you want."

"He's arrogant," Ferdi observed, as he and Norah egressed to the street. "He not only lies, but challenges you to catch him doing it."

A harsh wind had risen from the northeast, bringing with it an end to the spell of mild weather.

"There's a lot of tension between those two," Norah went on.

"He inhibits her," Ferdi said.

"Yes and no. There's a struggle going on, and I'm not sure over what. Yesterday at the morgue, Carmen was forthcoming. She told me the whole story about how Dolores got pregnant; how upset the family was; how she went home to be with her sister when she gave birth, and then brought her and the baby back. She indicated it was a temporary arrangement till Dolores could pull herself together and decide what to do. I got the feeling Carmen wanted the arrangement to be permanent. Maybe she was even planning adoption." She paused. That could be a subjective reaction, Norah thought, and didn't pursue it further. "Today she didn't say a word about either of them—except as regards funeral arrangements."

"I doubt Herrera would have agreed to adopt. He's sure not showing any sorrow for the victims," Ferdi remarked. "In fact, I think Carmen's grief is getting on his nerves."

* * *

Early that Sunday morning, while the sun was still bright, as though to bestow a particular blessing upon the inaugural, the police swept the entire area around Federal Hall for terrorist devices. After which, the public was guided through metal-detector gates and allowed to enter. Those scheduled to march in the parade, wearing the breeches, white stockings and perukes of two hundred years ago, formed up. Dignitaries took their places on the specially constructed stands.

Will Barthelmess hadn't wanted to go. The recent developments in the campaign had first raised his hopes—and Judith blamed herself for that; she should never have mentioned the possibility of the endorsement—and then dashed them. Withdrawing from the three-way race, Lorne Nicolson had not only withheld his support from Barthelmess, but had thrown it to his opponent, Roy Sieghle.

"If you don't show up, you'll give Nicolson's endorsement more importance that it actually has. People will say you're a bad loser."

"A loser is a loser; good or bad doesn't make any difference," the congressman retorted as he packed his suitcase in the bedroom of their expensive suite.

"What have you lost, actually?" Judith wanted to know. "The support of a man who couldn't make the run himself? What could he have thrown your way—a few unpaid volunteers? We have plenty of our own. His campaign staff? His PR people? We've already got better."

"Money. His financial backers. Now they go to Sieghle."

"Who says? There's no guarantee that the money will go with the endorsement," she reasoned. "You let Ralph and me worry about that, all right? For God's sake, you haven't lost. Not yet. This is the time to show you're a fighter. You've got to appear at every one of today's functions. Roy Sieghle will, you can bet. Are you going to let Sieghle have the nomination by default?"

Chief of Detectives Luis Deland was at the Federal Hall ceremony, but Bureau Chief James Felix was not, although he had been scheduled to attend. Quietly, Felix set to work to organize two parallel task forces; one in Queens, headed by Detective Sergeant Paul Rittenhouse, a member of Felix's staff, and the other in Manhattan, headed by Detective Simon Wyler, Lieutenant Mulcahaney's choice. As agreed upon in the conference early that morning, the purpose was to gather those witnesses who had been present at each shooting and remained cool enough to be able to give a description of the perpetrator when it was all over. These would be brought together with a police artist for the creation of a portrait of the suspect in each shooting. Armed with the portrait, the forces would spread out a second time seeking identification.

At Felix's behest, without regard for overtime, they worked into the night, but it was soon evident to the team commanders, Rittenhouse and Wyler, that the descriptions from each set of witnesses were not compatible. There was the natural distortion of memory caused by time. The ability to observe and recall in greater or lesser degree differed from witness to witness. These differences were not glaring within each group but marked between them. It was decided to call in a second artist and make two drawings.

By five Sunday afternoon, the sketches were ready. The first depicted a man with dark, heavy jowls, needing a shave. His soft visored cap was pulled well down over small eyes that were too close. The second was thin, bearded like Fidel Castro, and wore dark glasses. Simon Wyler tapped on Norah's door and placed both on the desk in front of her.

She studied them closely. The first, the sketch of the man who allegedly shot the Amerasian children, showed that he was stocky, and according to the accompanying description, not more than five six and weighing about a hundred and eighty pounds. The weight could be padding around his middle; the jowls could be wads of cotton inside his mouth. The second drawing showed a man with a beard and dark glasses, a more obvious disguise. Witnesses said this man was at least six feet tall, maybe more. Lifts in the short one's shoes couldn't have got him up that far.

Judging by the portraits, the men could be anywhere from the late twenties to early forties in age.

Wyler tapped the second portrait, the one of the man with the heavy beard. "According to the kids who saw him in the firehouse, this is the man."

"Then this is the one we go after," Norah said.

There being nothing that needed her personal attention, Norah decided she could go home. She was tired and depressed, one condition aggravating the other. Lately, she'd felt a lack of motivation. She wasn't sure whether she needed a medical checkup or a change in life-style. As was happening so often lately when she was in an emotional slump, she thought of Randall Tye.

Once home, Norah changed into an old, comfortable pair of gray slacks, red T-shirt, and rubber-soled flats. From the stack of TV dinners in the freezer, she took the top one without even looking to see what it was and put it in the microwave. When it was ready, she did take the trouble to turn it out on a plate and brought it to the living room, where she set it on the coffee table in front of the television set. She tuned in to the Liberty Network News. Randall was just coming on.

As anchor, he went through the news of the day with his usual mix of seriousness and charm. At the twenty-five-minute mark, he launched into what he called his Essay.

"Once again tonight we are faced with an example of the collapse of law and order in our city and in our society. Yesterday, while most of us were proudly celebrating the heritage of a free people by watching either in person or via television the stately procession of tall ships down the East River, a man armed with a semi-automatic AK-47 rifle opened fire on a group of citizens at a school playground in the heart of Manhattan. A sixteen-year-old girl and her infant son of five months were murdered. Thank God there were no other casualties. But because there were no other casualties, the police are saying this was no random shooting. They say it was a private murder committed on a public street. But so far they have found no motive. Isn't it more likely that this atrocity was one more skirmish in the drug wars which have turned our streets into battlegrounds? Up to now these shoot-outs have been restricted to the outer fringes of our metropolis. We've rationalized that people should know better than to jog in the park at night, or stroll along the waterfront on a hot summer's eve, or in the East Village, or Harlem, or Brooklyn. We've been willing to relinquish these territories. And now must we also beware the Upper East Side? Where do we draw the line—three blocks from Park Avenue? Is it too late to draw the line? Do we arm ourselves and barricade our doors? Do we move away and abandon the city? If so, where do we go?

"Maybe the shooter was carrying out a personal vendetta against the young mother and her child, but the arrogance of the attack out in the open in front of witnesses at high noon indicates total contempt for the laws of our society. That contempt is fostered by drugs. Drugs cause a moral breakdown."

The camera closed in on Randall Tye. His amber eyes seemed fixed on each and every individual viewer. They were filled with sadness and with regret. "I say that if the killer acted under the influence of drugs, then whoever supplied him is as guilty as if he himself had pulled the trigger."

The camera held the tight shot, and then there was a quick fade to black.

Norah turned off the set. No use trying to reach Randall. She knew what it was like immediately after the show went off the air—a sudden release of tension, everyone talking at once, the switchboard swamped with calls. Tonight it would be extra hectic, Norah thought. Later, after he'd had a couple of beers and something to eat, Randall would start to wind down. Then he'd remember their date and he'd call her. Unless it was very, very late—in which case he'd call her in the morning.

But she was wrong. Randall Tye called within the next fifteen minutes. He was still charged up. She could hear it in his voice.

"So. Did you catch the show?" he asked straight out.

"Yes." Norah hesitated. "It was very effective."

"But?"

"Not everything that happens in this city can be blamed on drugs. There are other stresses, other motivating forces."

"Not in this case. I don't think so."

"Do you know something we don't? Do you have information we don't have?"

"Only what logic dictates."

"Not specific evidence?"

"Oh, for God's sake, girl, if I had any kind of real evidence that could lead to an arrest, I'd tell you. You know that."

"Okay."

"Anyway, that's not why I called." He paused. "I've got big news. You know I was in the process of renegotiating my contract? Well, I've just heard from my agent—the network has agreed to our terms. I'll be making top dollar. I'll be making more than any anchor on any network. It's all to be announced at a special dinner day after tomorrow. I want you to be there with me."

"Congratulations. That's wonderful. I'm very happy for you, Randall." *You deserve it,* was the next thing she should have said, but somehow she couldn't. In this last broadcast he had put himself in opposition to the police and so to her. Maybe he believed he performed a service, but in the sense that it had also catapulted the network into acceding to his demands, it was self-serving. If she were to point that out, he would reply that he had merely given the story a slant, that he was not the only reporter on television or in the press to do so; that was the way the game was played. If she argued that it was manipulative, he would agree but not see anything wrong in it. They had been over this before.

"So the dinner is this Tuesday. I'll pick you up at seven-thirty. Okay?"

Nothing about tonight. He'd forgotten the date, apparently. "I'm not sure I'll be able to make it, Randall," Norah replied.

"You don't have to be on call around the clock. You can spare a couple of hours. Felix is handling the canvass, isn't he?"

It never ceased to surprise her how much he knew and how quickly he got the information.

"Come on, Norah."

"I'd like to be with you, but if something comes up . . . "

"It won't."

"Do your sources tell you that?"

"My bones tell me. It's going to be my night, Norah. I want you to share it with me."

Nothing about getting away to the mountains, either.

Chapter _____
_____SEVEN

Almost as soon as she'd hung up, the phone rang again. It was Jim Felix. Under his customary calm, she sensed excitement. "We've got several IDs on Identikit Number Two," he told Norah, using the designation for the flea-market shooter. We've got an address. He's not home, but the building manager verifies that he lives here. We've got two men downstairs and two on the roof. We're putting outposts around the block."

That didn't sound as though he were merely delegating, Norah thought, and felt her own blood race.

"You want to come over?" he asked.

"You bet."

Norah drove the silver-gray Volvo down the FDR Drive to the Brooklyn Battery Tunnel, entering as the sun was setting and emerging on the Brooklyn side in twilight. Montague Street wasn't far. She was familiar with the Brooklyn Heights, Cobble Hill area. Montague was a quiet, residential street, comprised of recently renovated brownstones, newly planted trees, and window boxes displaying stately late-season tulips in a variety of colors. Its principal attraction was the vicinity to the Brooklyn Heights Promenade, a long terrace walk overlooking the harbor and the tip of Manhattan with its distinctive and awesome skyline. At this hour the sky and water were a luminous blue. The streetlights had just come on. Not a place in which a crazed killer would be likely to make his lair.

The people who lived here, either in the private homes or condos, had made monetary and emotional commitments to the community. They knew each other and shared each other's concerns. A stranger would be immediately noticed and commented upon, and, in these times, regarded with suspicion. The address Jim Felix had given Norah was of a large apartment building just across the way from the Promenade. Those apartments would not come cheap, and the people who lived in them would be as dedicated to the security of the community as the rest.

Norah made a slow turn around the block, ostensibly looking for a parking place, but actually checking for the police lookouts. If she hadn't been personally acquainted with three of the plainclothesmen she wouldn't have spotted them. She crossed the street to the rectory of the small church where Felix had set up to direct his stakeout team. On being admitted, Norah was shown to the rector's office which Felix was using as temporary headquarters.

"We've located the suspect's girlfriend," he told her. "Here, take a look at this."

She knew the face. She should; she'd been studying it since Simon Wyler had handed her copies of the two portraits, trying to read into the eyes, the set of the jaw, the angle of the head, something of who each man was. Not possible when what she looked at was a third impression. Now she read the material that had been compiled.

Edward Corbin. Age twenty-eight. Single. Independent means. History of schizophrenia. Under private treatment combining medication and psychotherapy for six years. Parents deceased. Made provision for Edward, the only son, leaving enough money invested in blue-chip stocks and triple-A-rated bonds so that he could live comfortably on the income for the rest of his life. As backup, in case of unforeseen financial disaster, they invested in a small, well-established chain of pharmacies. Corbin received additional income from this, though he had no part in the management.

The apartment on Montague Street had been purchased six months before. The Board of Governors of the building accepted his application primarily on the basis of his financial standing. There was some trepidation regarding his medical problems but these were dispelled by the reports which unanimously attested to his complete recovery. Also, the real-estate market was very soft at the time. Buyers of Corbin's financial reliability were not numerous.

It didn't say so in the report, but Norah knew that in most such cases mental good health depended on continuing and faithful use of the prescribed medication.

She looked up to indicate she was finished reading. At that, Felix went to the door and looked into the shabby reception room. "Miss Racik? Will you come in, please? I'm Chief Felix and this is Lieutenant Mulcahaney. Sorry to have kept you waiting." He waved her to a chair. "Can I get you anything? Coffee?"

"No, thank you." She sat nervously at the edge of a low-slung chair, whose bottom had sprung, probably afraid that if she sat well back she'd have trouble getting up again.

Gertrude Racik wasn't particularly attractive, but her coloring was striking. Her eyes, almost lashless, were a brilliant blue. Her hair was a flaming red, pulled back into a magnificently thick ponytail. She was older than she appeared at first glance, Norah decided, well into her thirties.

"I don't know what I can tell you," she began defensively, before they had even asked. "Edward and I only went out together a few times. He didn't confide in me. He's not ready for a relationship."

"You lived in the same building he does, Miss Racik, isn't that right?"

"I used to when I lived with my parents, but I have my own place in TriBeCa now."

"I understand prices are very high there. You must have a good job," Felix remarked.

She smiled. "Not that good. I share with two other girls."

Felix smiled back. "How did you happen to meet Edward Corbin?"

"It was Sheila's turn to have the apartment to herself for the weekend, so I was spending it with my parents. I went down to the basement laundry room Saturday morning. I was behind Edward in line for a machine. We got to talking."

"And one thing led to another?"

"It looked like it might. We saw each other several times over the next few weeks, had dinner, took in a movie now and then, went for walks along the Promenade, and then . . . that was it. I invited him for dinner at my parents' and that was a mistake. He said okay, but at the last minute he canceled. After that, even the casual dates stopped. I called a few times, but he said he was busy. Busy doing what, for God's sake? He doesn't have a job. He doesn't have any hobbies. He said he'd get back to me when he had time, but he never did. I asked him what was bothering him, but he insisted nothing was bothering him and hung up. I didn't really believe that and I thought I could help, so the next Saturday I came over and went down to the laundry room and waited for him. As soon as he came in and saw me, he knew what I was there for and he was angry. Very angry. He turned red. He yelled at me. He said he'd tried to let me down easy, but since I was too dumb to take the hint, he'd tell me straight out: He didn't want to see me anymore. I thought for a second he was going to hit me."

Tears brimmed in her eyes. "Sorry, but that's all there is."

"How did your parents feel about your friendship with Corbin?" Norah asked.

The witness studied her new questioner. "How should they feel? I'm thirty-five years old." She paused. "All right, I'm thirty-nine and I've never had a serious boyfriend. Edward's nice-looking, single, and he has private means." The eyes of the two women met with understanding. "He was quiet and polite to my parents when he called for me. He brought me home early." Gertrude Racik sighed. "Naturally, when we stopped seeing each other, they were disappointed. But then Edward started to act strangely. He took to wearing an army uniform, complete with those heavy, round-toed, laced boots. He prowled the neighborhood. Everybody in the building was talking about it, but nobody knew what to do."

"Was he wearing a beard?" Norah asked.

"I never saw him with a beard," Gertrude Racik replied. "The point is, he wasn't bothering anybody. In fact, to the contrary. There'd been some teenagers loitering on the block, some of them dealing drugs. There were about eight of them in the gang. One day, Edward walked up to them. Nobody knows what he said, but they haven't been seen since."

"When Edward approached this gang, was he carrying a weapon?"

"I wasn't around, but my parents say yes. He kept acting more and more strange—going out mostly at night, disappearing for a couple of days and when he showed up again it was in uniform and with the automatic under his arm. Everybody was getting very nervous. It was like living with a time bomb and not knowing when it would go off. The board decided they didn't want him in the building anymore, but how could they get rid of him? He owned the apartment. What could they do?"

"They should have reported to the police."

Gertrude Racik was silent for several moments. "They were afraid."

Felix and Norah exchanged glances. If the guy was wandering around in a uniform he got from a costumer, say, and with a semi-automatic he could have got almost anywhere, why hadn't he been spotted by an RMP and picked up? Maybe he had.

The radio receiver on the desk crackled.

"He's just entered the perimeter, crossing Montague and heading toward the building." The lookout's voice was low but charged.

"Armed?" Felix asked.

"Looks like an AK-47."

Popular weapon lately, Felix thought. "Okay. Nobody moves. Let him get inside and up to his apartment," Felix enforced the orders already given. He turned to the girlfriend. "Miss Racik, you'll wait here, please. It shouldn't take long."

She nodded, her face chalky. "What are you going to do to him?"

"Nothing, Miss Racik. We're just going to take him in for questioning."

Gertrude Racik's brilliant eyes shifted to Norah. "They won't hurt him, will they?"

The perimeter was pulled in closer and tighter around the building. Once the suspect was in and had entered the first of two elevators, two detectives from outside joined those already hidden in the lobby by the service door. The pair took the second elevator up to the suspect's floor. Felix and Norah came from the church and went up, then the power was turned off.

Simon Wyler reached for Corbin's doorbell, pushed it, and drew back quickly. He waited, then reached, rang, and pulled back again.

"Who is it?"

The voice came from the back. Simon looked to Chief Felix and got the nod.

"Police, Mr. Corbin. We'd like to talk to you."

"What do you want?" The voice was closer now, coming from just behind the door.

"We just want to ask you a few questions, Mr. Corbin. Open up, please."

There was a slight pause, then the chain rattled indicating its disengagement, bolts were turned—two of them—and the door opened inward. Edward Corbin stood squarely in the middle of the opening, a perfect target.

He faced them—an assembled force of five men in plainclothes and one woman—and without being told, raised his hands.

They looked him over. Edward Corbin was six feet tall, thin, and his brown hair was conservatively styled. But he was clean-shaven rather than bearded, as in the Number 2 portrait, and he didn't wear glasses. These were superficial details, Norah thought. It was the expression on Corbin's face that bothered her. In the portrait there was cunning; this man was bewildered. It was her experience that the witness's feeling toward the suspect was reflected in the description he gave and thus came through in the artist's drawing. Still . . .

The suspect stepped back and the police entered his apartment. Wyler patted him down while his partner on the team covered him.

"He's clean," Wyler pronounced.

Nevertheless, Boyle kept the .38 Police Special on him.

"Where's the weapon?" Wyler asked.

"What weapon?" For a brief moment the suspect was almost convincing.

"Come on, Corbin, we know you have an AK-47. You've been brandishing it all over the neighborhood."

"Oh. Oh, that. Sure." His expression cleared. "I'll get it."

"Hold it!" Wyler snapped and his partner's gun was rock steady. "Don't move. Just tell us where it is."

"In the bottom drawer of the bureau." He nodded over his shoulder toward the bedroom.

They waited, frozen, eyes fixed on the suspect while Wyler went in. It was a large room but sparsely furnished. There was a double bed, a chair, nightstand, and, of course, the bureau. Just to make sure, he checked the nightstand and the closet before going through the bureau, the bottom drawer of which held soiled shirts, shorts, socks. Under them was the weapon. He picked it up and gasped.

He carried it out and handed it to Jim Felix.

"It's a toy."

Norah looked at it. Everybody looked at it.

"Is this what you've been terrorizing the neighborhood with?" Felix asked.

No wonder Corbin hadn't been picked up and no "unusual occurrence" report filed, Norah thought.

"I'm not the one terrorizing the neighborhood," Corbin replied.

"Are you sure there's nothing else?" Felix asked Wyler.

"Not in the bedroom, sir."

"Do you mind if we take a look around, Mr. Corbin?" Felix asked. They had a warrant, but under the circumstances it paid to be polite.

Corbin shrugged and lit a cigarette.

The "look around" was thorough. The men were experienced and knew every possible hiding place. They went through every closet and piece of furniture, the kitchen cabinets, the stove, and the refrigerator. They tapped walls and examined joints in the parquet floors. In one spot where the floor had buckled, they loosened the glue and lifted up a section one foot square. Nothing. Except for that piece of parquet, when they were through there was no indication a search had taken place.

Edward Corbin lit one cigarette after another till it was over. "Satisfied?" he asked Felix.

"I'm satisfied you have no weapon on the premises, Mr. Corbin, but I'm not satisfied as to why you've been roaming the neighborhood dressed in that costume and carrying a replica, an exceptionally well made one, of a deadly weapon."

"This 'costume' is the battle dress uniform of the U.S. National Guard."

"Where did you get it?"

"It was issued to me when I joined. I wear it to and from the Armory on Sixty-seventh Street in Manhattan for the same reason police officers wear their uniforms to and from the station house—to reassure citizens and put some fear into the punks. Ask around, you'll find I'm getting better results than you are."

"Where were you on Saturday, March eighteenth, at noon?" Norah asked, very much aware of what the narrowing of Felix's green eyes portended. The date was known to every officer in that room.

And, it seemed, to Corbin as well. "That's when the Amerasian children were shot, isn't it? I was on maneuvers with my unit, the 107, supporting the Second Brigade, at Camp Smith. We left Friday night and returned Sunday at two P.M."

There wasn't much point in asking the next question, Norah thought, but she did, anyway. "Where were you yesterday at noon?"

"Same place. At camp. Same schedule. We go once a month."

Chapter_____

_____EIGHT

Fiasco.

The weekend for which Judith Barthelmess had such high hopes lay in a shambles around her. It had taken all of her persuasiveness to get Will to fulfill the schedule which had been planned to give the appearance that he was riding a rising wave of support. He'd tried; she had to give him that. He'd put on a good show, but somehow it wasn't convincing. The other man, Sieghle, acted as though the nomination were already in hand. The host and the hangers-on fawned over him. Everybody on the bandwagon! The quicker you jumped, the greater the rewards later. That's the way the game was played, Judith thought bitterly. Everybody knew it. Despite his efforts, Will had remained out of it.

Before leaving for the airport and the trip back to Washington, Judith Barthelmess called Ralph Dreeben.

"Are you still with us?" she asked with a lump in her throat.

"Now, Judith my girl, what kind of question is that? I wouldn't think of jumping ship," he intoned unctuously.

He couldn't, she thought, of course not. They were tied to each other irrevocably. She wished she could rely on his support as being freely given, but she'd known what she was getting into when they made the deal. Now they both had to stick by each other like it or not.

"What do we do now?" she asked.

"You do what you've been doing so expertly all along—sell more real estate."

"I don't like it. I'm getting nervous. Also, I think Will is getting suspicious."

"I don't see why he should, unless you've let something slip."

"No. But if he ever finds out . . ."

"Don't let him find out," Ralph Dreeben concluded firmly and hung up.

Fiasco.

The phone was ringing as Norah walked into her office. She caught it just in time. It was Randall.

He knew, of course. By now, everybody in the media knew. Communications had been conducted over the regular police frequency; there had seemed no reason to go to the trouble of using land lines to keep the operation secret. So now the word that the police had mounted a big stakeout and ended up with the wrong man had gone out and spread like wildfire. It would get a big play for sure. PR was already struggling with damage control. But it wouldn't do much good. From her own recent experience, Norah knew it was close to impossible to divert a dedicated reporter from a hot story. She could even anticipate the "spin" the various journalists would put on the affair. Some would stress the hard work that had led to identification of Edward Corbin as the likely shooter, and the ensuing disappointment. Others would suggest the police had not done a thorough job of investigation and had wasted time and manpower and frightened the people of Brooklyn Heights. Some would heap ridicule on the officers in charge and treat the whole thing like a farce.

Had they gone in too soon? Norah asked herself yet again and once more set aside the doubt. No way she was going to second-guess Jim Felix. His team gathered enough background on the suspect to go in. Since the neighbors weren't talking and the RMPs on regular neighborhood patrol had not filed a report, they might have had to tail Corbin for weeks before stumbling on his National Guard affiliation. Unless they picked him up on one of his self-styled "tours," how could they have known he was playing at vigilante with a toy gun?

"I'm sorry, Norah," Randall Tye said. "These things happen. It wasn't anybody's fault."

"Thanks, Randall."

"But I still think you're going about it the wrong way."

"Please, I thought we'd agreed . . ."

"Right, we did. The thing is I'll have to comment on it and . . ."

"You've already warned me. You've told me over and over that you think the case is drug-related. Fine. That's your opinion. It's your job to say what you think, so go ahead and say it. I don't care. You don't have to clear your material with me. None of the other anchors do." As soon as she'd said it, she was sorry. She could almost see Randall flinch. It had been uncalled for, and yet she couldn't take it back.

"Why are you so touchy about this?" Tye asked.

"I'm not touchy," she flared. "Okay, I guess I am. I don't know why."

"I'm trying to be fair, Norah."

"I know that."

There was a pause during which each one sought to express the thoughts that weighed heavily in their minds and on their hearts, but remained silent.

Randall Tye gave up first. "So, I'll see you Tuesday night, right?"

Norah took a deep breath. "I don't think so. I really don't feel like partying."

"It's not a party. It's a testimonial. It's the celebration of a promotion. Like if you were being appointed Captain. I'd be with you then. I want you with me Tuesday. It's important to me, Norah."

She felt a hot flush course through her whole body. "It's important to me, too," she said quietly with all the sincerity of which she was capable.

Randall had accused her of being touchy, and it was true, Norah admitted. So far, she was following one line of investigation, the private lives of Dolores and her baby and Carmen and Juan Herrera. It was just about played out. Carmen would be leaving soon for Puerto Rico and the funeral. Herrera, under surveillance, had so far not made a false move. It was time to listen to some gossip.

Most apartment dwellers in Manhattan would not recognize their next-door neighbor if they should happen to meet him on the street. The more elegant the building, the more insulated the tenants. Norah believed that the building in which the Herreras lived was different, perhaps because the residents shared the same ethnic origins, and because a large proportion of them had lived in the building since its construction. Norah guessed they would be well informed about each other; the difficulty would be to get them to talk, especially to the police.

The building had already been canvassed, and Norah went over the reports once again. The one on Mrs. Imelda Martín, who lived on the same floor as the Herreras, appeared promising.

The first thing that struck Norah when she called on Mrs. Martín was the run-down condition of her apartment, especially in contrast to that of the Herreras. The Herreras' place had been freshly plastered and painted and equipped with the latest appliances. Mrs. Martín's bathroom ceiling was cracked, ready to fall; wall tiles were missing; the toilet tank hung high above the bowl and had a pull chain. The kitchen, too, was hopelessly old-fashioned. Mrs. Martín, however, did have one modern appliance in her bedroom—a new, late-model Singer sewing machine.

Samples of her work were everywhere—ruffled curtains on the windows, slipcovers on everything. There was a stack of neatly folded quilts on a chest against the wall, and one spread out on the machine.

"Did you make those?" Norah asked. "Beautiful," she commented at Mrs. Martín's shy nod.

"I sell them in the flea market."

"Oh?" That hadn't been in the report. "Were you present when the shooting took place?"

"No. I stayed home that day. I wasn't feeling so good." She was in her seventies and walked with a cane. Her gray hair was thin and the pink scalp showed through. Her eyes were either rheumy or she cried easily. Or both. They filled now as she thought back to the events of the morning. "Dolores Lopez offered to take my place at the stand and sell my quilts, but I said no, thank you. She pretended to be so nice and so friendly, but she wasn't nice. She pretended to love that little baby, but she didn't care about him. Not even a little."

"Why do you say that?"

"Because it's true."

"How do you know?" Norah pressed, but gently, always gently.

"She resented the baby. He tied her down. She couldn't go out and have any fun. She was only a young girl, after all."

"Her sister says she wasn't interested in dating or making friends. She says Dolores was devoted to the child."

The old woman shrugged.

"Why should she lie?" Norah pressed.

"That is what she believes. Or wants to believe. I know different. I saw Dolores slap the baby when he cried, slap him hard. Another time she put the pillow over his face to silence him. She was sitting with him in the carriage in the nursery section of the playground. I was nearby, sewing. 'What are you doing?' I yelled, and right away she pulled the pillow off. I went over. The baby was red in the face, but he was all right."

"Did you tell Mrs. Herrera?"

"No." Tears welled up. "How could I? *Dios mío!* I wish that I had."

It certainly wouldn't have been easy, Norah thought, and most likely she wouldn't have been believed. "How did Mr. Herrera feel about having his sister-in-law and her child living in his house?"

"I have no idea."

Norah thought she had no more to say, then suddenly Mrs. Martín blurted, "He works long hours at his garage. It was nice company for his wife." She shot a sideways look at Norah.

Norah wasn't sure what she was intended to understand from that. For the moment, she set it aside. "Did you observe Dolores Lopez lose her temper with her baby on any other occasion?"

"No."

"Every mother loses her temper with her child occasionally, but it doesn't mean she doesn't love him."

"Have it your way, lady."

Imelda Martín sat down to the machine, spun the wheel, and stepped on the electric treadle. She bent her head to the work.

The next witness Norah had chosen to interview on the basis of the DD5s was a Mrs. Hope Winslow, who lived in a red-brick, middle-income apartment project directly across the street from the garage on York. She ran a day nursery. As soon as she got off on the second floor of C Building, Norah could hear the sounds of children. She had to ring twice and hold the second ring a long time before someone called, "Coming!"

It took a while longer for Mrs. Winslow to appear. When she opened the door, she had in her arms a three-year-old girl with blond pigtails and a boy of the same age at her knee. The girl was sucking on a lollipop, and the boy was reaching up to snatch it away from her. Mrs. Winslow was dusky, with a lovely open face, well-spaced dark eyes, soft, wavy hair, and full lips. She managed to remain serene, while keeping the two toddlers apart and ignored the noise of the other children romping in the room beyond.

"Mrs. Winslow? I'm Lieutenant Mulcahaney." Norah displayed her ID wallet. "May I come in?"

"Sure."

The vestibule opened into a big, sunny room. The floor was tiled; there were no curtains. The furniture, what there was of it, was scaled for children. The walls were decorated with their crayon drawings, grubby fingerprints, and a large blackboard. Hope Winslow gently pushed the boy away and then lowered the girl to the floor. "Now Gregory, you leave Melissa alone."

"She hit me."

"He tried to take my lollipop."

"Tell you what—I'll trade you two cookies for the lollipop, Melissa. Okay? And Gregory, will you take two cookies instead?"

"Okay."

Having confiscated the lollipop and dispensed the cookies, Hope Winslow grinned at Norah. "You need the judgment of Solomon with these kids."

"I'm impressed." Norah counted eight boys and girls, probably between the ages of three and six. "How do you keep your sanity?"

"I love it."

"Is there anywhere we can talk?"

"This way."

Hope Winslow showed Norah into a large, family-style kitchen. "We'll have to leave the door open. If I take my eyes off them for so much as a second—disaster. I don't know how they get into some of the predicaments, but they do."

Norah thought of Mark, the four-year-old she and Joe had adopted and then been forced to give up. "You must find it rewarding or you wouldn't be in the business."

"If you mean financially, I'm not getting rich, but in every other way that counts—you bet. Can I get you something—a cup of coffee, tea? Cookies, Lieutenant?"

"Coffee, if it's no trouble."

"No trouble if you don't mind instant. Actually, it's a treat to talk to an adult for a few minutes." With no wasted motion, Mrs. Winslow placed cups and saucers on the table in the center of the kitchen, spooned out the appropriate amount of freeze-dried, filled a saucepan with water and turned on the gas. "I've got some Danish . . . ?"

"I don't know."

"Come on, we only live once. Prune or cheese?"

"Cheese."

"Me, too. And damn the cholesterol."

The snack was served and consumed in companionable silence. Finished, Hope Winslow leaned back in the chair and sighed with satisfaction. "The only drawback in this job is that I can't have a smoke while the children are around. And that, I suppose, is actually an added benefit. So, Lieutenant Mulcahaney, what can I do for you?"

"I notice you overlook the York Garage."

"Hold it, Lieutenant. One of your people, Sergeant Arenas, was already around, and he asked me if I noticed anything suspicious over there, any comings and goings that weren't appropriate. I asked him and now I ask you—when do I have time to look out the window?"

"Your charges do go home at the end of the day, don't they?" Norah smiled.

The young woman smiled back. "Three of them don't. They're mine. And when the others leave, they remind me of how much attention I owe them."

"You're a lucky woman," Norah said.

"I know it. I'd like to help, Lieutenant, honestly, but there's nothing I can tell you."

"Maybe not. On the other hand, there could be something you've noticed and taken for granted but that could be of interest to us. Let's see if we can dig it out. Okay?"

"Okay."

"For instance—you get up in the morning—at what time?"

"Me? I get up at five-thirty, rain or shine, summer or winter," she replied promptly.

"So when you're in here fixing breakfast, you're probably aware whether the station across the street is open or closed."

"Oh, sure. It's open. The kid that works there, Perry, has done odd jobs for me—uncrating stuff, getting rid of cartons, like that, so I know he comes on at seven and opens up. The owner, he shows around eight or eight-thirty depending on what he's got in the way of repairs."

"You see, you know a lot more than you realized."

"How about that? Okay. Perry quits at three. An older man, Ace, comes on to pump gas till around eight when the whole thing shuts down. We've finished dinner and I'm stacking the dishes in the machine by then."

"Does Herrera close up or does he leave it for Ace?"

"Oh, he does it himself."

"Makes a pretty long day for him," Norah observed. "Almost as long as yours."

"The day will come when I'll be able to afford help."

"And you'll still put in the same hours."

Hope pursed her lips ruefully. "I guess."

"So. Let's see what else you can tell me. Did anything unusual ever happen across the street?"

"No."

"What kind of cars does Herrera work on—medium-priced, expensive, foreign, antique? Sometimes a garage is a hangout for idlers in the neighborhood. Anything like that?"

"Nothing like that at all. As a matter of fact, when we first moved here I was worried about characters hanging out, but Herrera discourages it."

"So no customer or visitor came around on a regular basis?"

"Not that I'm aware of. Except his wife and baby, of course. I thought it was so sweet that they were still enough in love for her to go there to be with him."

"Do you know Mrs. Herrera?"

"No."

"Then how do you know that's who it was?"

"I assumed . . . What other woman would visit regularly and bring an infant?"

"Did you ask Perry who the woman was?"

"I wasn't that curious, Lieutenant. Now . . ."

"What?"

"I wonder . . . She came so regularly. Except for real bad weather, heavy rain or snow, she didn't miss. There were some mighty cold days when I thought the baby shouldn't be out no matter how well bundled up."

"How frequent were these visits?"

"Every other day. Again, Lieutenant, there might have been times I didn't know about."

The sink was directly in front of the window. Standing there, Norah could get a good view of the drive-up and pump area and the shoe box–shaped building that housed the hydraulic lifts. She could see the plate-glass front of the office, but the reflection made it impossible to discern who or what was inside. She assumed there would be additional space at the back for storage, rest rooms, or private quarters. How much of what was going on back there did Herrera's employees, Perry and Ace, know? With the boss on the premises, it was no time to go over and ask.

"How long on average did the visits last?"

Hope Winslow shook her head.

In the act of unhooking the nozzle, Herrera raised his head, and it seemed to Norah that he was looking at that very window. Even if it were so, he couldn't see her, couldn't know she was there. He couldn't have seen her drive up because she'd taken the precaution of parking around the corner.

"Can you describe the woman who came with the baby?" Norah asked.

"Not from here, Lieutenant. During the winter she wore a bright-red storm coat with a hood. Recently, she had a blue cape and a white sombrero."

Hiding and at the same time calling attention to herself. Interesting.

"I had the feeling she was young," Hope Winslow said. "Real young. Maybe I got it from the way she moved and how she handled the carriage. She was not careful with the baby."

The affair, if indeed there was one, had been conducted brazenly, Norah thought. Almost as though they wanted people to know. But how could that be?

When she left, Norah avoided the garage, but did not return to her car, either. She walked around aimlessly. There were several construction projects in the area. The largest was on Third and Sixty-eighth, on the site of what had been the New York Foundling Hospital. It had been torn down to make way for another luxury condominium. Work was well along—the foundation excavated, and the debris long since carted away. In smaller, less well-funded projects, the Dumpsters might remain on the site for weeks, even months.

It was getting late; she had to dress for Randall's dinner, so she found a phone and called the squad. She told Ferdi to get a team and check the construction projects in the area of the lab.

Chapter
NINE

During what Norah thought of as her celebrity period, she had accumulated a wardrobe to suit every occasion. She wouldn't need to go out and buy clothes for at least the next five years, she thought as she made her selection. For Randall's dinner she would wear the beige satin, long, slithery, high at the neck and bare in back. It was simple, yet rich. It suited her, and it was appropriate. She supposed she would be sitting on the dais with Randall and she wasn't too pleased about that, but all eyes would be on him; her presence would have little importance.

The affair was held in the Waldorf Astoria ballroom and attended by five hundred of Randall's friends and colleagues, by network big shots from the president to the executive vice presidents of News, Special Events, Sports, Entertainment, and so on down to Tye's own news staff. As far as Norah could tell she was the only representative of the police department—correction, she was there in her private capacity as the honored guest's girlfriend. Norah looked at Randall beside her, handsome in white-tie, and then out at the people who had come to honor him and be honored by his invitation, and she felt proud.

The speeches began. Brief, witty, written by specialists and delivered by specialists. A film, *The Randall Tye Story,* depicting the popular news anchor's career, was next on the program. After that, the man of the hour himself would speak.

The lights dimmed; music swelled as the screen was lowered into position and then Randall's face in a tight shot filled it.

Applause.

Norah felt a tap at her shoulder. A waiter was bending at her side, saying something, but she couldn't hear because of another round of clapping. He repeated into her ear.

"Phone call for you, Lieutenant. It's urgent. This way."

Keeping low so as not to break the shaft from the projector, Norah followed the waiter. All eyes were on the screen; nobody noticed. Outside the ballroom, she was shown to a small office.

"Mulcahaney," she said, picking up the phone on the desk.

"Danny Neel, Lieutenant. We found it. The baby carriage. We've got it!"

"Where?"

"Like you figured, Lieut, in a Dumpster right around the corner from the lab. It's badly charred. Looks like somebody tried to torch it, then either he couldn't get the fire going or he was interrupted. The Dumpster was handy, so he threw it in, expecting it would be buried under rubble and ultimately carted away."

He waited for some response, but Norah was silent.

"You want us to take it back to the lab, Lieutenant? Lieutenant?"

"I want to know everything there is to know about that carriage—who manufactures it, who sells it, who bought it and when."

"Yes, ma'am. But what should we do with it?"

"Take it back, of course. And tell them I want them to make sure it's only the baby's blood soaked into that mattress and nobody else's along with it. Tell them it's top priority. And tell them not to lose it this time."

"Yes, ma'am."

"Have you any idea how they managed to lose it in the first place?"

Danny Neel gulped. Norah could visualize his prominent Adam's apple bobbing.

"Somebody signed it out."

Norah felt a tight band around her chest contracting. "Who?"

"I figure he showed fake ID."

"Who? Let's have it, Detective Neel."

Neel sighed. "Ferdi. Sergeant Arenas. I figured we could clear it up and you wouldn't have to know."

Again Norah recalled the look on Ferdi's face when they reached the murder scene. He'd said that for an agonizing moment he'd thought it was Concepción lying on the pavement a few feet from the carriage with his son inside. That was the reason for his behavior. There could be no other. This time Danny Neel didn't break into her thoughts; he knew very well she was still on the line.

"You get the carriage to the lab. I'll meet you there. I don't need to tell you not to mention this to anyone—including Sergeant Arenas. Especially him."

After hanging up, Norah remained in the small office for several minutes. Somewhere along the corridor a door to the ballroom was opened and closed, and in the interval the magnified voices backed by a musical soundtrack reached her. The film was still on. Going back to explain to Randall now might throw him off stride for the speech he was due to make, she thought. She'd just leave a note. Under the circumstances, she had no choice but to go. Randall would understand.

Norah had not come in her own car but with Randall by limo, and she knew the limo was on hire by the network to be at Randall's disposal for the evening. He wouldn't be needing it for a while, so she told the driver to take her over to the police lab in Brooklyn. Once, during the months when she was working on the Valente case and first started dating Randall Tye, when she had been briefly a celebrity in her own right, Norah had shown up at a crime scene in all her unaccustomed elegance complete with a full-length coyote fur coat. She had felt terribly self-conscious and inappropriate, and had vowed never again to be caught like that, but . . . here she was. Only now she didn't care. Nor did it bother Norah one bit that she was using the network car and chauffeur, which she sent back when she reached her destination.

Norah swept into the antiseptic and institutional atmosphere of the lab and felt more at ease than she had at the party. The lab conducted every imaginable kind of examination of evidence: chemical (narcotics came under that heading); physical (automobile damage, broken windows, locks and keys, electrical appliances and so forth); personal marking for identification (fingerprints, foot and shoe impressions, teeth, laundry and dry-cleaning marks). Ballistics section handled comparisons of weapons and bullets and related shooting problems. Photography, ordinary and filter, infrared and ultraviolet light and photomicrography were important procedures. New and more modern methods were constantly being introduced, the latest and most impressive and far-reaching being the so-called DNA genetic fingerprinting. By whatever means, Norah had no doubt the lab would force the baby carriage to yield its secret. Of greater concern and urgency to her at the moment was Ferdi's alleged involvement with the removal of the carriage from the lab.

Danny Neel met her at the door.

"I want to see Sergeant Arenas's signature in the sign-out book," she told him.

"I've already looked at it, Lieutenant. It appears to be his."

"*Appears* doesn't mean a damn," Norah retorted sharply. "We'll get an expert on it. Next, I want to talk to the clerk on duty when the evidence was signed out. I want a description of the officer and I want to know exactly what was said. And don't tell me you've already covered that, Detective Neel. Don't tell me the description fits Sergeant Arenas. Please."

So Neel remained silent.

"I assume you've noted the time of the sign-out and you've ascertained, subtly, Sergeant Arenas's whereabouts."

"Yes, ma'am. He was home with his wife."

They both knew this could not be considered a real alibi, although neither said anything.

"What we need to know, first and foremost, is *why* the baby carriage was taken. Are they working on it?"

Danny nodded.

"Good. I'll stay till they get results."

"Okay to stay with you, Lieu?" It was the first time Neel had ever addressed her by the casual nickname. "I might as well pace here as at home."

"Right."

She went over and sat on the nearest bench. Neel sat across from her.

Norah leaned her head back against the wall and closed her eyes. Thoughts, possibilities, tumbled in her head like clothes in a spin dryer. She must have dozed off because Danny had his hand on her shoulder and was shaking her gently. She opened her eyes. With Danny, there was a man in a white lab coat.

"You're finished?"

"Far from it, but we've got a preliminary report and I thought you'd want to know."

"Go ahead."

"We've found traces of cocaine inside the mattress, under it, and in the creases of the upholstery. We have no way of knowing how much there was originally, but there could have been a very large amount in bags sewn in there. In the hurry of retrieving them, it looks like one broke. What we have is the spill."

And that explained why they needed a double carriage for one baby, Norah thought, and why the carriage had to be retrieved—and fast. It did not explain why Ferdi was set up.

"How about fingerprints, hair, blood stains? Also, threads, fibers . . ."

"In due course, Lieutenant. The whole ball of wax, okay? But it's going to take a while. I don't think you should wait."

"What's your name?"

"Rest assured I'm not going to drop this job in favor of anything else, Lieutenant. Believe me, we've been getting plenty of heat on this, and the sooner I can hand in a complete analysis and you can collar whoever walked that perambulator out of here, the happier we'll all be."

Norah looked hard at him. "So tell me your name."

"Peter Rich, Lieutenant. Don't call me. I'll call you." He turned and walked back to wherever he'd come from.

"So, Lieutenant, can I give you a ride somewhere?" Danny Neel asked.

The wall clock showed one-thirty-five A.M. She'd left the Waldorf at a little before nine. Until this moment she'd forgotten all about the dinner and Randall. Of course, it was much too late to go back. By now it was all over.

"Thanks," she replied to Neel. "I'd appreciate a ride home."

Norah half expected to find the limo parked in front of her house with Randall in it. It had happened before. But not this time. She thanked Danny and went upstairs, again half expecting Randall would be in the upstairs hall at her apartment door. But he wasn't there either. Obviously, he was annoyed, she thought as she put the key in the lock and walked inside. After turning on the lights, the first thing she did was check her answering machine. No messages.

He was angry. He shouldn't be, Norah thought. He wouldn't be when she explained about Ferdi. Maybe she should call him?

She dialed and listened to the ringing. He didn't answer and his machine didn't cut in. That was being childish, Norah thought and after at least a dozen rings, she hung up and started for the bedroom. But if she went to bed now she wouldn't be able to sleep; she'd only brood. Why not go over there? Why not straighten it out now? If she went to bed without talking to him she'd be behaving as childishly as he was.

The night doorman at Randall's building was new. She gave her name and he tried to get her to wait while he called upstairs and announced her, but she kept on going to the elevators. By the time she got to the penthouse and rang the bell, Randall was probably just answering the phone. Nevertheless, it seemed an overly long wait. When he finally came to the door, he was in pajamas, bleary-eyed, hung over. She'd never seen him like this.

"What can I do for you, Lieutenant?"

"Oh, for heaven's sake, don't take that attitude, Randall. I'm sorry for what happened, but it wasn't my fault."

"It never is. Forget it."

"Randall, I apologize."

"Fine. Accepted." He pulled back as though to shut the door on her.

"I admit I was wrong."

"How can that be? You're never wrong."

Norah flushed and swallowed the hurt. "Are you going to make me stand out here in the hall, or are you going to let me in so I can tell you what happened?" She couldn't help but add with some tartness, "Unless you already know."

Randall's sluggishness lifted. He glanced over his shoulder and shrugged. "Come on in."

Norah marched to her usual place at the end of the sofa, but he made no move to sit beside her. He stood in the middle of the room.

"All right, I'll say it again, Randall; I'm very sorry for leaving your dinner. What came up was a big break in the case. I had to go and I had to stay longer than I anticipated." She hesitated. Should she mention Ferdi's possible involvement? Whatever interpretation Randall might put on it, the speculation wouldn't do Ferdi any good.

"Why?"

"There is a drug connection, just as you thought."

Randall's puffy, tired eyes glinted. "What changed your mind?"

Again, Norah hesitated. She cared about this man and trusted him, but she also recognized he was subject to the stresses and demands of his job as she was to hers. "We found the baby's perambulator. It contained traces of cocaine."

Tye formed a silent whistle. "Who found it and where?"

"Detective Neel. In a Dumpster not far from where it was taken." By now every reporter on the police beat knew that much, she thought, and would soon know the rest. "The carriage was signed out by Ferdi Arenas."

"It's obvious that whoever did it, it wasn't Ferdi. And I'm not just saying that to please you."

"Thanks, Randall."

"No cop would be dumb enough to sign out a vital piece of evidence using his own name."

"Well, thank you very much."

"Sorry. I was trying for a little humor."

"This is hardly the time for humor."

"Right. You're right. Whoever did it was instructed to use Ferdi's name by someone who knows the two of you work together closely."

"That's no secret."

"The intent was to get the evidence and also to distract you. It has distracted you, hasn't it?"

"Oh yes. And I'm not going to forget it." Nor would Internal Affairs, she thought, once it came to their attention. She intended to make sure Ferdi was in the clear long before that. It shouldn't be hard—a handwriting expert declaring the signature in the property log a forgery should be sufficient.

"I don't believe they expected to cause any real trouble. They're playing a little game with you, showing you that they're one move ahead," Tye continued.

"Who's they?"

"The drug bosses." He let that hang for a minute. "One thing is sure —there was a big stash in that carriage or they wouldn't have gone to the trouble to get it back. They would simply have abandoned it and taken the loss."

Norah nodded.

"So Dolores was using the baby as cover and dealing from the carriage. Was Herrera supplying her? Were they both working for the same network? She could have been caught skimming, but it seems more likely that Herrera was using her to stake out new territory."

"I find it hard to believe a mother would use her baby like that."

"A baby she didn't want, remember. A baby that obviously cramped her style. Come on, Norah, getting pregnant doesn't automatically turn a young girl into a mother."

No argument, Norah thought.

Tye went on. "Look, a man armed with an AK-47 firing apparently at random manages to miss everybody but Dolores and her child. They had to be his specific targets and what other reason but drugs would there be for that kind of a public killing?"

Norah sighed.

"It's obvious that it was a contract killing."

"You're skipping too many steps," Norah objected. "For instance, did Carmen know? Did she suspect her sister and her husband were having an affair? Or did she think they were dealing? Was she part of the operation?"

"I'll build a foundation, don't worry."

"Not making wild guesses, you won't."

"You do it your way and I'll do it mine, and I'll bet you I get there first."

His eyes flashed; so did Norah's.

"I don't bet on the outcome of murder investigations."

"Lighten up, sweetheart. Let's call it a friendly challenge. What do you say?"

"It's not a game. I've told you that before. I can't stop you, but I would like you to stay out of this."

He appeared to be considering an answer when a crash, like glass shattered, came from behind the closed bedroom door. Tye winced. Norah froze.

After a moment, she asked. "Aren't you going to go and see if she's all right?"

"Oh hell, Norah, tonight was a big night for me. You shouldn't have walked out on me, not tonight."

"I didn't walk out."

"You never even bothered to call and explain."

"I left a note. Didn't you get it?"

"You considered that enough? A note left on the run? I thought I meant more to you than that."

"You do. My God, Randall, of course you do. There was no time. I'm sorry."

"Is this the way it's going to be? Are you always going to walk out?"

The bedroom door opened. A sultry brunette in a creamy satin and lace teddy, her hand held at her bosom and dripping blood, stood on the threshold. "I cut my finger, Randy."

"Get her a bandage, Randy," Norah said and, turning her back, walked out.

"What did you expect?" he yelled after her. He was pale, sweat oozed from every pore. "What the hell did you expect from me? You're the ice queen and I'm no saint."

Chapter TEN

Randall Tye awoke with a flannel mouth and a pounding head. When he managed, after considerable effort, to sit up and swing his legs over the side of the bed, a wave of nausea overcame him. He rushed to the bathroom and got rid of last night's dinner, maybe lunch, too. Legs trembling, he got back into bed. It rocked and pitched—a lifeboat in a stormy sea. He hadn't felt this lousy since his first network broadcast. He remembered it only too well.

Expecting to be nervous, he had taken a couple of tranquilizers prescribed by a doctor who was excited to have a television reporter, albeit one as yet not well known, as a patient. The Valium had calmed him all right, soothed him into a daze. Somehow, by a tremendous effort of will, he was able to read his cue cards and stumbled through the report. He thought he was through, his career finished before it had begun, so he went out and tied one on. The synergistic effect put him out for nearly twenty-two hours. He came to on the floor inside his own front door. It was lucky that no one at the station knew what had happened —based on his history, it would have finished him. His debut might not have been auspicious, but it wasn't the disaster Randall thought, either. After that Tye promised himself to stay off drugs of any kind and to limit the booze. His discipline was strong enough so that he was able to do it—till last night.

What had made him lose control?

Not Norah's leaving the dinner to respond to a summons involving one of her people. Had the cases been reversed, he would have done the same. The excitement of the event? The honor accorded to him by his peers? That wasn't new to Randall; he thrived on adulation. Could it be he cared more about Norah Mulcahaney than he realized? Once again she had shown him that she put him second in her life, and he had tried to show her it didn't matter and had succeeded only in showing her that it did.

He groaned and closed his eyes. He dozed off and when he woke a second time, he felt better, relatively. He was able to get up and make it to the kitchen to fix some black coffee. He wished Georgina hadn't appeared while Norah was there. Of course, Georgie had shown herself on purpose; she'd known exactly what she was doing. The whole embarrassing scene replayed in his head. Then he recalled the argument over the case and the dumb challenge he'd thrown down. He'd been out of line and he should call Norah and apologize for that. He remained convinced that the flea-market shooting was part of the drug wars, but he should not have set himself up in competition. He reached for the kitchen wall phone.

But he didn't dial. Suppose he did investigate? Suppose he solved the case? That would be humiliating for Norah. He didn't want that. But if he could help? Tangibly help, not merely by offering theories but by bringing in actual evidence? If he had a share in breaking the case, wouldn't Norah be grateful? Then would she acknowledge they could work together, be a team? Wouldn't that show the relationship could be mutually beneficial?

Suddenly, Randall felt a lot better. He popped a couple of aspirins in his mouth and washed them down with the rest of the black brew. He dressed and went to his new office: actually, his old office expanded and lavishly redecorated as befitted his new eminence. As he walked briskly through the newsroom, he acknowledged the greetings from those who had not attended the dinner; they were looking to see how he would handle himself and what demands he could make on them now that he was top anchor in the business. Georgina Llewelyn was careful not to behave differently, nevertheless he sensed a special quality as she said hello, first raising her eyes and then lowering them. He also knew they were being observed.

The incident last night had begun innocently when they stood together under the Waldorf's canopy, he waiting for his driver, and she for the doorman to get her a cab. Tye's driver came first, of course, and uncharacteristically—he was not known for consideration of those of lower status, and as an assistant stage manager Georgie was just about anonymous—he had offered her a lift. Someone might well have observed them leaving together and started gossiping. Or else the girl herself was spreading it around.

"See you in my office, Georgie." Though Randall smiled and held the door for her, letting her pass through first, it was not a request.

"Get home okay? Sorry I couldn't take you myself, but I had a little too much of . . . everything."

"Sure." Her eyes were fixed on him.

It struck Tye that she was not trying to profit but was, in fact, uncertain about her own status. "Look, I had no right to put you in the middle of a situation between me and Lieutenant Mulcahaney. I apologize for the embarrassment."

She looked very different this morning in her work clothes which consisted of loose pants and tunic. She wore no makeup. Her long dark hair hung straight, showing off a perfect oval face that needed little embellishment. She was a Botticelli come to life. Until she spoke. Then a nasal twang destroyed the image.

"As long as you didn't do it on purpose."

That stunned Tye. "On purpose?"

"Yeah. Like you knew she was going to show up."

"You think I asked you to come home with me just so Norah could find us together?"

He considered. The suggestion was not that outlandish. In fact, he might subconsciously have done just that. How about Georgina's motive? Did she expect to get booted and was this her defense? In other words, try and kick me out and I'll tell my side.

"No, Georgie," he said. "You're a beautiful woman. I'd had a few too many and my intention was to take you to bed. Considering how much I care for Norah Mulcahaney, it's as well it didn't happen. On the other hand," he bowed gallantly, "I wish I had."

A slow flush suffused her face. "Me, too." She shrugged. "So that's it? That's the end?"

"There was never a beginning," he pointed out gently.

"Right," she nodded and walked out.

For a moment he felt a pang of real regret. Only for a moment. Then Randall Tye settled himself in his old chair at his old desk in the new modern decor. The file on the flea-market shooter was at hand. He opened it and for the next hour was oblivious of all else.

* * *

Norah left Randall Tye's apartment confused, embarrassed, and hurt. What could she expect after all, she asked herself. She had told him up front that she was not prepared for a sexual relationship outside marriage. When he promptly offered marriage, she had put him off. She had no right to demand that he remain celibate.

Wrung out physically and emotionally, Norah looked forward to a deep and heavy, all-obliterating sleep. But sleep eluded her. She kept playing the scene with Randall over and over in her mind. She tried to concentrate on their discussion of the case, but despite her best efforts the shapely, nearly naked brunette kept intruding. Had Randall used the girl to make her jealous? No, he was too decent, too straight for that. Oh hell! Norah thought, I *am* jealous. I can't help it, I am. What's the matter with me? I love this man, but I can't commit to him. Why am I resisting? We squabble every time we're together, and it's my fault. What am I trying to prove—to him or to myself?

Randall had been right about one thing, Norah acknowledged as she punched the pillow and turned over: the shooting was drug-related. It was evident that the comings and goings Hope Winslow had observed from her kitchen window did not indicate an illicit affair between young Dolores and her brother-in-law. At least, sex was not their principal bond. Coke was. The coke was transported in and distributed from the baby carriage. The money collected was stashed there and delivered to Herrera. The baby was the perfect cover.

Norah recalled how boldly and openly he had asked what happened to the baby carriage, and how obligingly she had told him. What he'd wanted to know, of course, was who had the dope? Forging Ferdi's signature was both a clever and a show-off way of getting it back.

Would a charge against Herrera stick? Not for five minutes, Norah thought as she turned over on her other side. Naturally, Herrera would deny any knowledge that drugs were being sold from the perambulator. Any half-bright paralegal could get him off. Only Dolores could have been charged, and she was beyond the reach of the law. She was no longer a risk to her own gang, nor a threat to a rival organization.

The next thing Norah knew, her phone was ringing. Startled, she sat up. The room was rosy with the early-morning sun. The digital clock on the nightstand showed 7:32 A.M. She must have forgotten to set the alarm. Then she remembered this was her day off, or supposed to be. Meanwhile, the phone was still ringing.

"Mulcahaney."

"Dr. Worgan's office, Lieutenant. We were trying to reach you yesterday evening. Dr. Worgan is out of town . . ."

Phil was attending a conference of pathologists, she remembered. In Boston? Rochester?

"He wanted you to be advised that the autopsy of Dolores Lopez revealed she never bore a child."

Norah was stunned into silence.

"Lieutenant? Did you get that, Lieutenant?"

"Yes, I did. Yes, thank you. Oh, one thing. Have the bodies been released?"

"Yes, right after the autopsies were completed."

As Chief Medical Examiner, Phil Worgan could hardly handle every case personally. Even if he'd done the two autopsies himself, there was no reason not to release the body of Dolores Lopez. As for the baby . . .

"Was Mrs. Herrera informed of the findings?" Norah asked.

"Sorry, Lieutenant, I don't have that information. I do know that Mrs. Herrera claimed both bodies."

Carmen had been pressing to have them released, and in Worgan's absence someone had goofed and let her have them. Earlier on Norah had found the urgency natural. She wasn't so sure now. She needed to talk to Carmen.

They lived only a few blocks apart. Norah got up, dressed, grabbed a cup of coffee, and walked over.

Carmen Herrera was gone.

"She didn't waste any time," Norah remarked.

Herrera merely shrugged.

There were plenty of questions Norah wanted to ask him, but she decided against further interrogation at this time. Her silence might bother him more. Instead, she made arrangements to keep him under surveillance.

Randall Tye had a source in the ME's office, and he received the information about the autopsy result not much after Norah. He wasn't quite sure how to use it.

Whose baby was he?

It would make a great lead, but where did you go from there?

By mid-morning, Tye, with a camera crew, was ready to descend on the building in which the Herreras lived. He had the documented blessing of the Mayor's Office of Motion Picture and Television Production. He possessed a legal permit to film. He had the presence of Officers Rubinstein and Perrota to enforce his rights. He knew from experience that he would stir up the neighborhood and provoke a reaction from his target, and that was precisely his intention.

He arrived in working clothes: slacks, turtleneck cotton shirt, foreign-intrigue trench coat, collar turned up. He beamed the full force of his charm on the assembled crowd and individually on those he interviewed. And he interviewed many more than he had any intention or possibility of using. But they didn't know that. When the segment was aired, they would be disappointed, but for now they ushered Tye into the building like a conqueror.

At first, Juan Herrera refused to answer his bell.

"I'll get rid of the cameras," Tye negotiated through the door. "We'll talk privately. Or else we can wait. Sooner or later, you're going to have to come out. We'll be here. You can count on it."

"You can wait till hell freezes over," Herrera replied.

Tye hadn't expected that. He was stymied, temporarily. Nobody in the hallway moved or spoke. Minutes passed. The truth was that Randall Tye couldn't afford to stand out there for long. The flea-market shooting was a big story, but not the only one he was covering.

"Suppose I tell you that the autopsy reveals Dolores never bore a child?"

Another silence, not so long this time. Then the sound of the bolt being turned, and the door opened partway.

"No cameras," Herrera warned.

"No cameras." Tye waved the crew back and stepped inside.

Herrera faced the reporter, arms slightly bent and fists clenched, balancing on the balls of his feet: a fighter sizing up his opponent. He was short, but he was strong, and Randall was not looking for a physical confrontation. Skirting Herrera, he entered the sun-filled room beyond. Like Norah, he was interested in the indications of money.

It intrigued Tye that whereas the druglords at the top of the chain lived in opulence, in obscene extravagance, flaunting their riches, the middlemen did just the opposite. Most continued to reside in low-income neighborhoods in modest apartments, careful not to draw attention to themselves.

"Are you sure about the baby?" Herrera asked.

"Doctors don't make mistakes like that." He waited, then added, "I wouldn't lie to you. It would be pointless."

"Worse than pointless."

Tye took it as it was intended to be—a warning—but he didn't understand why Herrera was so affected. "Were you having an affair with Dolores?"

"What?" Herrera actually laughed. "You must be crazy."

"Did your wife know what was going on?"

"For God's sake, man, there was nothing going on."

"Mr. Herrera, the girl was seen visiting you at the garage three or four times a week. She brought the baby in its carriage. You weren't just discussing the weather."

"I shouldn't have let you in here. It was a mistake."

"Traces of drugs were found in the baby carriage. It looks like your sister-in-law was dealing and using the excuse of taking the baby out for a stroll to make her rounds. Now give me a reason why she was going to see you."

"I don't have to give you a reason for anything. I have nothing to do with drugs. Nothing. I don't deal. I don't use. That's it."

"How about your wife? Did she know what you and Dolores were up to?"

"How many times do I have to tell you? We weren't up to anything. If Dolores was involved with drugs, Carmen didn't know and I sure as hell didn't!" His dusky skin was suffused with crimson. Tye wondered whether he had a heart condition or whether it was the price of self-control.

"When is Carmen coming back?" he asked. Then took a chance and added, "Is she coming back?"

Herrera took several deep breaths. His color gradually returned to normal. "Of course, she is. Next week. She's coming back next week."

Danny Neel regaled Norah with his version of Randall Tye's descent on East Sixty-ninth Street.

"He got a bunch of interviews with the neighbors, but Herrera refused to let the cameras into his apartment."

Norah didn't laugh. "Herrera did talk to Tye? Privately?"

Neel nodded.

"We'll have to listen to the broadcast to find out what he got. If he's ready to go public . . . which he may not be. Meantime, what did you get?" she asked.

Neel shook off a growing uneasiness. "The word is Mrs. H. is coming back next week."

"So soon? Who says?"

"That's what Herrera's been telling the neighbors." The detective consulted his notebook. "But Mrs. Martín, the seamstress who lives on the same floor as the Herreras, claims Carmen told her she was never coming back."

"Is that so?" Norah murmured. Carmen Herrera had given strong indication to her that she didn't want to come back. "Maybe she meant to that apartment?"

Neel warmed up. "Right, right, Lieutenant, that's what I think. The talk is that Herrera's giving up the place and moving out of the city. He bought a house somewhere on the Island."

The money must be piling up, Norah thought. "If it's true, we need to know where the house is located."

"Should I find out how it's being financed?"

"You're way ahead of me, Danny."

"Never, Lieut." He grinned, displaying a fine, even set of teeth and a dimple in his chin.

Norah sat awhile organizing what she knew and the arguments she intended to present, then she called Jim Felix's private line.

"According to the autopsy, Dolores Lopez never bore a child," she told him.

He mulled it over. "So, what do you think?"

"The baby was Carmen's. Who else's?"

"And the father?"

"That's the question. Carmen's gone back to Puerto Rico with the bodies. I have a feeling that if we want to talk to her, we should hurry."

"You think she's in danger?"

"I'm getting mixed signals. She's coming home; she's not coming home. The Herreras are moving out of the city; nobody knows for sure when or where."

"That's not much to go on," Felix pointed out. "She did say she'd spend some time in P.R. And it is understandable that she wouldn't want to come back to that apartment."

"I'd like to go down and talk to her," Norah said. "It's a short trip. I could go and be back the same day."

Felix considered. "You know I respect your instincts, Norah, but the trip isn't justified, not on what you've told me so far. Let's wait awhile."

And Norah, who usually argued her causes fiercely and tenaciously, hesitated. Was she really afraid for Carmen or was she anticipating Randall's next move and trying to beat him? Doubting her own motives made her uncharacteristically compliant. "Whatever you think."

It took Felix aback and caused him to offer more than he'd intended. "Let's wait till next week, then we'll review the situation."

It was on the tip of Norah's tongue to say she could fly down on her own time and at her own expense, but once more she questioned her own motivation and remained silent.

Chapter ELEVEN

Randall Tye didn't need to ask anyone's permission to go anywhere. He told the network news director what he intended to do, though he did put it in the form of a request. Of course, it was instantly granted. The next morning, the news anchorman was on a Pan Am flight to San Juan. A helicopter was standing by to transport him directly to the hotel landing strip in Mayagüez. A suite had been reserved for him at the Hilton and a rental car placed at his disposal. He had turned down the chauffeur. He didn't want anybody to know what he was up to and was only too well aware that no matter how much you paid a man for silence, someone would pay him more to talk. There was a road map in the glove compartment, but he didn't need it to get to the town—all he had to do was turn right at the exit from the hotel grounds and follow the main road.

It was three in the afternoon when Randall Tye drove into Mayagüez's main plaza. Like every Spanish town, this was the core of activity—religious, commercial, social. It was dominated by a church. There was the usual park with dusty palms that offered little relief from the sun. In the larger cities, San Juan and Ponce, the siesta was a thing of the past, but here it was still observed. As Tye parked his rental car, Mayagüez was waking from its midday torpor. The metal shades over the small *tiendas* were being rolled up; chairs and tables set out in front of the *restaurantes* and *cafés* were quickly filled. School children in blue and white uniforms headed back to class. The banks and professional offices located on the side streets that radiated from the Plaza Central were unlocking their doors.

The waiting room of Dr. Carlos Morales was already filled. The nurse receptionist sensed that Randall Tye was someone important. Although she didn't recognize him, he had little trouble convincing her to get the doctor to see him. The doctor had never watched his program either; however, Dr. Morales accepted Tye's credentials and listened attentively to his account of the shooting of Dolores Lopez and Baby Charlito.

"I understand you delivered the baby," Tye said.

"That is so."

"In the hospital here in Mayagüez?"

"No, in the mother's home. That is to say in the home of her parents. The mother was not married."

"Doctor, according to the autopsy done in New York, Dolores Lopez never gave birth."

"There must be some mistake."

"Yes, I think so," Tye agreed pleasantly. He had come prepared for just this. "Here is a photograph of Dolores and this one is of her sister, Carmen. Which one did you attend?"

There weren't enough roads at that end of the island for him to get lost, Randall Tye thought as he turned off what passed for a paved road, potholed and rutted, onto a single lane dirt track through fields of sugarcane so high it was like going through a tunnel. Even so, he began to wonder if he hadn't taken a wrong turn after all. Unable to see anything ahead or behind and barely a patch of deepening blue above, he felt swallowed by the cane. After thirty minutes of jolting bumps, he was thinking about turning around if he could find a place to do it when a field of cane, burned to blackened stumps, opened the view and he saw the Lopez hacienda gleaming rosy in the setting sun.

The house was constructed of concrete, two stories, with a series of arches on the ground floor. It was surrounded by at least half an acre of trimmed lawn. Through a ring of royal palms he could glimpse the bay of La Parguera, whose waters on a moonless night threw off phosphorescent shine.

Most Puerto Ricans who leave their beloved island for the mainland do so with the firm intention of making a fortune and coming back to enjoy the fruits of their toil. Few succeeded in either intent, but most did share what they earned with the family they left behind. Having put his trained and ruthless research team on Juan Herrera, Tye already knew that the only family he had here was by way of his wife, Carmen

Lopez de Herrera. He also knew that Carmen's people were poor, seasonal workers in the fields. Now they owned a substantial portion of the very fields in which they once labored. There was little opportunity on the island to amass the kind of money needed to build such a house and to buy and maintain such a property. The money had to come from the mainland. According to the look of the place, it had been coming in large quantities and for some time.

Randall Tye followed the drive bordered with red and white hibiscus and pulled up in front of a shallow flight of steps leading to the veranda which was festooned with purple jacaranda. As he got out of the air-conditioned car, the heat met him like a solid wall. He plunged through and by the time he reached the dark, well-polished, mahogany door, sweat covered his body. There was no bell, only a brass knocker. He pounded and the door opened almost immediately as though someone had been standing behind it waiting. Well, Tye thought, there was only one road to this place and apparently it was watched.

A young man blocked the entrance. He was in his mid-twenties, tall for a Puerto Rican, say six two or three. He had a broad chest and shoulders, narrow hips, and an intimidating aspect. "Yes?" he challenged.

The bulge under his ill-fitting jacket suggested a shoulder holster. Maybe the jacket was purposely ill fitting so the gun would be noticed. "I would like to speak with Señora Lopez de Herrera." Tye used the formal title in which the maternal appellation takes precedence and which was customary regardless of class.

It didn't impress the young man. "She's not here," he said and backed off to shut the door.

Tye moved one foot forward and braced himself. "When will she be back?"

The bodyguard, he had to be a bodyguard, looked down at the narrow, elegantly shod foot as though he would stamp on it and crush it.

"She went back to New York."

First, Tye was stunned, then angry that his source had failed to notify him and he'd made the trip for nothing. But it wasn't his custom to waste time in regret. From his wallet he drew a card and held it out. "Please present this to Señora García de Lopez." That was Carmen's mother. "Ask her if she would be so gracious as to spare me a few minutes of her time."

The young man took the card but stood there with it in his hand not knowing what to do. His instructions hadn't covered this.

"I'll wait," Tye said and, taking advantage of the momentary uncertainty, stepped across the threshold.

The physical act triggered an automatic physical response. He was pushed back. "You will wait outside."

But before the door could be slammed on him, a voice called from the shadowed recesses of the house.

"Está bien. Déjalo entrar."

The natural coolness of the thick walls and the soft cross current of breeze was instantly relieving; however, it took a while for Randall Tye's vision to adjust to the semidarkness and identify the woman who approached.

"Mrs. Herrera?"

"This way."

She led him into a small sitting room, gestured for him to sit, and then went over to a serving cart on which there were several glasses and a pitcher of something ruby rose with ice cubes in it.

"Sangría?"

"Thank you, yes. I can't think of anything I'd like better at this moment."

As she poured, Tye looked her over. She wore a plain black dress with a plain round neck, long sleeves, and a skirt that reached to her ankles. It made her look sallow and yet it suited her. Her dark curls had been brushed hard and pulled back and tied into a knot. This gave prominence to her eyes and pulled the skin at her temples tight, eradicating the few lines that were beginning to show there. He accepted the glass she handed him and drank almost half of it at one draught. "I had no idea it would be so hot here."

She didn't respond to his attempt at small talk. Instead, she sat down opposite him and came directly to the point. "What do you want?"

He met her look. Until that moment he hadn't himself known the precise answer to that. "I came to make a deal."

"What kind of deal?"

Deliberately, Tye finished his drink and then set the empty glass down. "What are you afraid of, Carmen?"

"I'm not afraid of anything."

"Then why are you hiding?"

"I'm not hiding. I'm here in my parents' house. How can that be hiding?"

"An armed guard answers your door. He says you've gone back to New York."

"You're not the first reporter who's come around trying to get a story."

"Surely you don't need an armed guard to protect you from reporters."

"My mother thinks so. She has lost one daughter and her only grandchild. I'm all she has left. Can you blame her?"

"She thinks someone wants to kill you, too?"

"She's scared."

"But you're not?"

Carmen Lopez de Herrera shook her head.

"Who's the baby's father?"

"I don't know. Dolores never told."

"Come on, Mrs. Herrera, let's stop playing games. According to the autopsy, Dolores never bore a child. The baby was yours. Obviously, you wouldn't have passed him off as your sister's if your husband had been the father. So who was it?"

She flinched. Her smooth, golden skin took on a bluish tinge. Her eyes narrowed and sparks shot through the slits. "I don't know what you're talking about."

"Why didn't you just pretend the baby was your husband's? Maybe you couldn't, is that it? Was Juan away at the time of the conception?" He watched her carefully as he considered the possibilities. "The baby was yours by another man. You could have got rid of it, that would have been the easiest solution, but you chose not only to have the child but to keep him with you. So what kind of a deal did you make with your little sister?"

"No deal. She was my sister and she was willing to help me."

"She was your little sister, your plain little sister, used to taking your leftovers, isn't that right? But she soon found out that this time she had the upper hand. Once she acknowledged the baby as hers, she was in control. You brought her up to the mainland and moved her and the baby in with you. Maybe you planned to adopt him later on, but for the moment you were content that your problem was solved. In fact, it was only beginning."

Tye paused. Carmen Herrera remained silent.

"It didn't take long for Dolores to see the kind of money drugs brought in, and she wanted some of it. So with Juan's help, she used your baby as a cover to deal. Every time Dolores took the baby out for a stroll in his carriage, she was carrying drugs, making sales, and delivering the take to your husband. And there was nothing you could do about it.

"Juan had been in the business a long time. He came up from street pusher to middle management. You knew. No way you could avoid knowing. You lived in comfort in New York. Your parents bought this place . . ." Tye spread out his arms to include the house and its land. "Where did the money for all this come from if not from Juan? And where did he get it? Not from running a gas station."

"The cane . . ."

"There's no money in sugarcane anymore. And now it seems Juan is moving up another level; he's buying a house out on Long Island."

It was only a twitch that broke the blankness of her face, but it was enough to tell him she was surprised.

"You didn't know?"

She studied the reporter closely. "You've asked a lot of questions. Why should I answer?"

"To avenge the death of your baby."

She was silent a while longer. "This house you say Juan intends to buy stateside, it won't be the first. And we won't live in it. He's bought other houses and we've never lived in any of them." With that, she rose and walked over to the bellpull. The bodyguard appeared promptly.

"Mr. Tye is leaving," she told him.

Night falls suddenly in the tropics. As Randall Tye drove back through the tall cane, the sun set and it was dark. Preoccupied with interpreting what he had learned and what he still needed to find out, he made a wrong turn and came out at the village of La Parguera. His Spanish was limited and nobody spoke English so that by the time he found his way back to the Hilton, it was after ten. He was tired, hot, and hungry. Nevertheless, he ordered the helicopter to take him back to San Juan and was extremely annoyed to learn the pilot wasn't awaiting his pleasure. That the landing strip was not to be used after dark made no difference to him. He wanted the pilot and his craft there and available. He had to settle for a takeoff at first light, which would get him to San Juan in time for the first scheduled flight to New York. Even Randall Tye had to admit that the circumstances did not warrant a special charter.

He had a couple of drinks before sacking down in his suite for the few hours before dawn. He rose calmer and took the trouble to use his well-known charm to soothe all those people he had alienated the night before. It wasn't enough to totally erase the memories of his tantrum, but he thought it was. He made his connection at San Juan with time to spare and relaxed at last in his first-class seat. He let the stewardess fuss over him while he planned his next moves. He foresaw no difficulty.

Upon arrival at JFK, the limo was waiting to take him home. Just twenty-four hours after he'd left, Randall Tye put his bag down and reached for the telephone to call the head of his research team.

"Liberty News, Higgins."

"Have you located the house?" Tye asked, having no need either to identify himself or to specify what house he referred to.

"Randall, hi! How are you doing?" the research chief responded cheerfully. "How is it down there? Hot enough for you?"

"I'm not down there. I'm back."

"Quick trip," Jeff Higgins commented, but having recognized the tone of his boss's voice, got down to business. "Yeah. It's in East Hampton. A regular mansion."

"Who's the agent?"

"Don't know yet. Since you didn't want to ask Herrera directly, or to use our police sources . . ."

"No, absolutely not. I told you."

"Right. Right. So we ran into a little trouble. We tried to contact the seller but he can't be reached. The house was offered through multiple listing, so we're checking."

"Good, Jeff, good." Tye mollified Higgins who was, after all, one of the top people in the field and on whom he relied heavily. "I hear that Herrera has been involved in other real-estate transactions."

"Interesting," Higgins murmured.

"Isn't it? Whether he always used the same agent or worked with various agents, is one of the things we need to find out."

"Right."

"We can't assume he was limiting himself to the area around the Hamptons, but it's a place to start. So I want a list of all the agents carrying this particular offering on their books. Have it ready. I'm coming over."

Randall hung up but kept his hand on the receiver. He should call Norah. He had opened a new line of investigation. So far he had only a hunch as to where it might lead, but he wanted to tell her, share what he had learned. Still, he hesitated.

Norah must know Herrera was buying a house, he thought. Up to now they'd both had the same information, more or less. It was a question of what each of them did with it. Wasn't that the idea? So he would follow up, get the name of the real-estate broker, talk to him, and then, depending on what came of that, he would present it to Norah. He took his hand from the receiver. As soon as he did, the phone rang.

"How was Mayagüez?" Norah asked.

He felt himself flush. He hadn't hidden the trip from her, but he hadn't called to tell her, either. "Hot," he replied.

"And what did Carmen have to say? Did she admit the baby was hers?"

"More or less."

Norah sighed. "Randall, please, let's stop this stupid competition. If you've got new information, you've got to tell me."

Randall wavered. He wanted to confide in Norah. He knew he could trust her not to leak the information to his competition, but she was not a free agent. She could be forced to share what he told her with her superiors and a secret shared was not a secret for long.

"Look, Norah, I'll make a deal with you."

"No more deals."

"Listen to me. I may be on to something big; I'm not sure. I have to look into it. But I'll put a time limit on my investigation. Two days. In two days at . . ." he consulted his watch, "twelve-fifteen, I walk into your office. I've either got the case solved or I turn everything over to you and withdraw."

"I like the last part," she said, "but no. Absolutely not. This is kid stuff, Randall. It's theatrics. Are you planning to announce the name of the killer on your show?"

"You're kidding, I hope. I have some integrity."

"All right, then. I'm coming over."

Tye wanted to see her. He wanted to work with her, not in competition. "No. No, I won't be here. Two days, Norah. Trust me."

* * *

Tye knew that Norah wouldn't let it go at that. Though he'd told her not to come, she was probably already on her way, and he wanted to be gone by the time she arrived. He called Jeff Higgins.

"Have you got that list?"

"Ready and waiting."

"Bring it to Frank's." That was a favored hangout on Sixth, a couple of blocks from the studios. "Twenty minutes. And don't tell anybody." That last was unnecessary but he said it, anyway.

Tye had been looking forward to a shower and a change, but he couldn't take the time. He had released the car and driver that had picked him up at the airport, and he turned down the doorman's offer to get him a cab.

"It's a nice day for a walk," he said and set out with his habitual long stride, but once out of sight, he hailed the first available taxi.

Higgins was waiting for him at their regular booth at the rear. Without preliminaries, he handed over a sheet of paper. Five real-estate companies were listed.

The newscaster glanced down the column quickly. "Have you checked any of these?"

Jeff Higgins was a thin, intense man in his mid-forties, sandy-haired and nearsighted. He had met Randall when they both worked on *The Green Mountain Press,* a small Vermont weekly. As reporters, there had been a friendly rivalry between them. Then Tye shifted from the written to the spoken word and began his climb to fame. Jeffrey Higgins rose also, but more slowly and in a more limited field. He was Associate Editor when Randall called and offered him the job as head of his research team at Liberty. Higgins hadn't hesitated.

"The first two," he replied. "Parker Realty and Prestige Properties each received an inquiry regarding the listing, but before they could show the house, it was withdrawn from the market."

"How about the other three?"

"I've put Koslow and Jones on them."

Randall frowned. "This one," he pointed to the next to last name. "Executive Transfers, that's Washington based, isn't it? It deals with CEOs and government appointees who need to find new homes and maybe get rid of old ones."

"Right."

"Have they got a branch here in New York?"

"No. They have an 800 number."

Tye pursed his lips as he thought about it. "I can see the owner listing with them, but why would Herrera buy from a firm in Washington, D.C., when there are several local, making the same offering? It's interesting."

"Very," Higgins agreed and their eyes met. "You want me to go down and look into it?"

"No, I'll do it myself."

Higgins reminded him that the show had been switched from Saturdays to Fridays.

"Stoddard can stand in for me."

Jack Stoddard was an ambitious and undeniably charismatic addition to the news staff. He was also obviously out to undermine Tye and to maneuver himself into as many of the top man's assignments as he could. That Tye was willing to let him sub on *People in the News,* his most prestigious program, was an indication of how important he considered the Herrera case.

"Are you sure that's a good idea?"

Randall grinned. "Give him a chance to hang himself. If he doesn't, I'll have to come up real big. And I will. Don't I always?" Randall got up. "When Lieutenant Mulcahaney comes around asking for me, you can tell her . . . tell her I'm out house hunting." He grinned. And that was how he would present himself to Executive Transfers, as a man on the verge of marriage, buying a house as a surprise for his intended.

Would Norah be pleased if he actually did buy a house? Would she consider it an indication of the seriousness of his intent?

When Randall hung up, Norah had called him right back. He didn't answer. He couldn't have left that quickly, she thought, but he'd be gone for sure by the time she arrived at his place. She went anyway. The doorman didn't know where he'd gone, only that he'd set out on foot. Probably to the studio, he suggested; *People in the News* was on a new night.

Yes, she knew that. If she went to the studio, they'd tell her he was rehearsing. So she went back to the squad, where there were two new cases that claimed her attention and took precedence over Randall's game.

Norah worked at her desk till *People in the News* went on the air. She tuned in via a small black-and-white set in the office and was stunned to discover Randall replaced. Norah called the station instantly without waiting for the show to end. She wasn't the only one. The station was inundated with calls, and Norah had to wait her turn. Finally, she got through only to be told Randall Tye was on special assignment. When she identified herself to the operator, she was put through to Randall's secretary, who told her the same thing.

"Come on, Emily," Norah appealed. "Come on. This is police business. I need to know where he is."

"Lieutenant, I swear to you I don't know."

"When will he be back?"

"I don't know that, either. When the assignment is concluded, I suppose. I'm sorry."

"You must know where to reach him in case of emergency, for heaven's sake. He's not in a war zone!"

"I can't contact him. Not unless he calls in."

Norah was angry. "All right. When he calls in I want to be notified." Her blue eyes blazed. Her chin was set.

Chapter

TWELVE

Forty-eight hours, Randall Tye had stipulated. Within two days and two nights he would either solve the case or turn over the information he'd gathered. If anything could get Randall back before the self-imposed deadline it would be the performance of Jack Stoddard, Norah reflected as she watched the rest of the *People in the News* show on Friday. Whether or not Stoddard was using material prepared by and for Randall, which he must have, Norah thought, he managed to deliver it with a personal flair, to impart a unique sense that it belonged to him. He had a light touch which contrasted effectively with the serious aspects of the story and at the same time underscored his compassion. He was never heavy-handed. At the end of the program, he paid a gracious tribute to Randall Tye, stated that it was an honor to stand in for him, and thanked the viewers for not turning the dial. He said nothing about when Tye would be back. The next night, Stoddard handled Tye's regular segment of the evening news. This time he made no comment about the absence of the regular anchor.

By mid-afternoon Sunday, Randall should have been back, but Norah didn't hear from him. He wasn't scheduled to go on the air Sunday night. She decided to wait till Monday, though she did so with considerable unease. On Monday morning she went directly to the studio.

Everything appeared normal, Norah thought as she stood at the door of the newsroom. Nobody paid any attention to her; every person there was preoccupied with the particular segment of the news that was his responsibility to process for public consumption. The only difference—and once she noticed it, Norah was very much affected—was that Randall's usually wide-open door (he liked to work with the clacking of the typewriters and ringing telephones and chatter as background) was closed. People scurried by without so much as a glance. Emily Flower sat at her desk just outside.

"He's on special assignment, Lieutenant," she reiterated. "He doesn't make a habit of checking in at fixed intervals." Her light-hazel eyes were fixed on Norah. While her voice was firm and loud enough to be heard by everyone, her eyes transmitted anxiety for Norah alone.

"He was due back yesterday," Norah pointed out.

"I don't know anything about that, Lieutenant. He didn't tell me when he'd be back. He didn't tell me he was going."

"He must have told somebody," Norah insisted. "The News Director must know. Where's his office?"

"Mr. Pace is on the thirty-third floor." The secretary lowered her voice, "Try Jeff Higgins, head of research. They work very closely. He's at the far end of the hall." She bent her head and resumed typing very rapidly.

Norah headed in the direction Emily had indicated. The door at the end of the hall was open and led into a small reception room. A young, pretty, overweight woman wore earphones and frowned in concentration as her beautifully manicured fingers flew over the typewriter keys. Norah had to place herself in direct line of vision to get her attention. She stopped typing and removed the headset.

Norah displayed her ID. "Where can I find Jeff Higgins?"

"That way. Second door."

She waited till Norah got to it, then nodded to encourage her to enter. Immediately after that, she replaced the headset and got back to work. Nobody goofed off. Impressive, Norah thought and went on with her own business.

"Mr. Higgins?" she asked the thin man in shirtsleeves sitting at the cluttered desk surrounded by stacks of files. "I'm Lieutenant Mulcahaney, Homicide." Once again, she displayed her ID.

"Yes, I know. I prepared background for your first appearance on the show. Randall did his own workup the second time you were on. What can I do for you?"

"You can tell me what Randall's up to."

"Don't I wish I could! Nobody knows that, Lieutenant. I'd say you're probably better informed than the rest of us."

"Then I wouldn't be here asking, Mr. Higgins. I'm tired of the pretense that everything's all right. Randall was supposed to be back yesterday. Nobody seems to know where he went or why he hasn't come back. Doesn't that concern you?"

"I've known Randall for a very long time, Lieutenant. He plays a lone hand. He's been in some tight spots, but he knows how to take care of himself."

"This time it's a little different. He's withholding information from the police. And I'm beginning to think you are, too."

"Why don't you give him another day or so? I think the reason we haven't heard is that he's on to something and he wants to make sure to wrap it up before coming in."

"What? What is he on to? I'm going to make it very unpleasant for you and for the network unless you tell me."

Higgins shrugged. "Randall said you'd come around. If you did, I was to tell you that he's out house hunting."

"House hunting?"

"He wants to surprise you."

"Are you trying to make a fool out of me, Mr. Higgins?"

"Oh God, no. I apologize, Lieutenant. I think, now that I look back, I think that was a kind of clue he left for you . . . just in case."

Norah pulled up a chair and sat. "You'd better tell me what this is all about."

She listened, looking over the list of real-estate agents Jeffrey Higgins handed her. "Have you made any effort in the last twenty-four hours to find out if Randall did in fact contact any of these people?"

"He said he was going to Washington first."

"Yes, I can see that he would, but that's not what I asked you."

"I'm sorry, but I think you're making too much of this. I can't believe he's in any danger."

"I'm not interested in what you believe, Mr. Higgins. I want answers."

Higgins's pale eyes flashed. For a moment it looked as though he would refuse. Then the fire was banked. "I did contact Executive Transfers early this morning. I was told Randall had been there and that he'd talked with a Miss Judith Ancell. That was late Friday afternoon."

"And then?"

"I tried the other agencies. Randall was never in touch."

"So his last known contact was this Miss Ancell."

Higgins nodded, then lifted one shoulder. "That's her maiden name. You might know her better as Judith Barthelmess, the wife of Representative Will Barthelmess, who is now running for the Senate nomination."

Norah stared.

"I should have told you sooner."

"That's right, you should. What else are you holding back?"

"Randall had information that Herrera was trading in real estate."

"Through Mrs. Barthelmess?"

"That's what he went to Washington to find out."

"All right, all right. He interviewed Mrs. Barthelmess at the real-estate office in Washington, D.C. He hasn't been seen since. I'm going to rule out accident; Randall is a nationally known personality, if he'd been in an accident or admitted to a hospital, he would have been recognized and the network notified."

"Exactly." Higgins was relieved. "So nothing's happened to him. He's got a lead on a big story and, forgive me, Lieutenant, he doesn't want you to get in his way."

Norah suggested to Jim Felix and Manny Jacoby that an interview with Mrs. Barthelmess in Washington could be interesting. Both agreed. After arranging with Ferdi to cover the chart in case she should be delayed getting back, Norah drove out to LaGuardia, put her car in the lot, and caught the two P.M. shuttle.

It was not her first trip to the Capital, nevertheless Norah felt a thrill of pride as they circled the familiar monuments before landing. She took a taxi directly to the Georgetown home of Representative and Mrs. William Barthelmess; Judith Barthelmess worked out of her home and that was where Randall had called on her.

Today was Monday. The House was not in session. Norah had checked and learned that though the congressman would not be in town, his wife would. It suited her. However, she had not requested an appointment, preferring not to give Mrs. Barthelmess the opportunity to duck the visit, although that wasn't likely. Both Felix and Jacoby had agreed.

Georgetown was a prestigious address renowned over the nation and the world. To live here meant not only high government and social position, but money. These historic, but small, cramped houses were exorbitantly expensive, either to buy or rent. In spite of that, there was a long waiting list. The Barthelmess house was on a tree-shaded street still laid in the ancient cobblestones; its sidewalk was worn brick. Norah paid off the cab and climbed the stairs to a recessed front door with a fine, old brass knocker. She was scrutinized through the peephole before the door was opened.

"Yes, ma'am?"

The girl who asked was young, dark-haired and fair-skinned. She wore a plain gray dress with long sleeves and a white collar and cuffs. Though it had no apron, it was evidently a maid's uniform.

"I'd like to see Mrs. Barthelmess, please."

"Who shall I say is calling?"

She spoke with a marked brogue. Norah had the impression the girl served in several capacities, one of which being to screen visitors.

"Tell her, please, Lieutenant Mulcahaney of the New York Police would like to speak to her." Norah handed the girl a card.

She wasn't impressed. She'd announced more important people, including the Speaker of the House and the Vice President of the United States. She admitted Norah into a tiny vestibule with a narrow stair directly opposite the door. "I'll see if Mrs. Barthelmess is in," she said and walked down to the far end of the hall, tapped lightly, and went inside.

Judith Barthelmess came out almost immediately and advanced toward Norah holding out her hand, along with a smile that was both cordial and curious. She had Norah's card in her left hand.

"Did you just get in, Lieutenant?"

"Yes. I came straight from the airport."

"I see. Well, can I get you anything? Coffee? Tea? A sandwich? What they serve on those flights isn't very satisfying."

"A few minutes of your time."

"Of course. This way."

Norah had seen pictures of Representative and Mrs. Barthelmess, and she had watched them on television. The candidate was handsome with a rawboned look that suggested he would be more comfortable with an ax in hand chopping wood than negotiating in the halls of government. His wife, with her thin, narrow face, and limp brown hair, had by contrast seemed colorless and retiring. In person, Judith Barthelmess evinced a great deal of charm, Norah thought as she followed her along the hall decorated with striped wallpaper and a slim, Federal-style console into a room that couldn't have measured more than ten by thirteen and was a combination sitting room and office. Mrs. Barthelmess waved her visitor to a comfortable armchair slipcovered in flowered chintz and sat across from her on the matching sofa. With this one move, she took the official sting out of the visit. Or tried to.

Settling back, Norah crossed her legs and went along with the informality, for now.

"I understand you had a visit from Randall Tye, the newscaster, this past Friday."

"Yes. He was interested in buying a house."

"Is that so? All the way out here in Georgetown?"

"As a matter of fact, no, not here."

Norah frowned. "I don't understand. If the house isn't in this area, why should he seek you out?"

"This house happened to be listed with us."

"I still don't understand."

"Executive Transfers is exactly what the name implies. We actually contact local agencies to search for properties outside our own immediate area. We even reach out overseas."

"You provide a service?"

"Exactly."

"This house that Mr. Tye was interested in, where is it located?" Norah asked, though she already knew the answer; Ferdi had not only located it, but had gone out to look at it and to talk to the neighbors.

"In the Hamptons," Judith Barthelmess replied. "Unfortunately, he could have saved himself a trip. It was already sold."

"That makes it all the more strange that he came all the way here."

Mrs. Barthelmess shrugged.

"He might have been interested in meeting you," Norah suggested. "You are an important person."

"My husband is the important one." She smiled disarmingly. "Actually, Mr. Tye said he was hoping to get married and the house was to be a wedding present. For you."

Norah blushed. "He mentioned my name?"

"It was also to be a surprise. It seems it is. I'm sorry that I've spoiled it."

"Who bought the house?"

"I'm not sure it would be proper for me to tell you."

"Why not? A title search has to be made and papers filed with the local authorities. That's standard, isn't it? So I can find out that way."

"You certainly can and with very little trouble, Lieutenant. I prefer not to be the one who gives you the information."

"Suppose I tell you I already know the identity of the buyer?"

"Then why ask?"

"His name is Juan Herrera. His sister-in-law and a five-month-old infant were victims in a recent playground shooting. You may have heard about it."

"There are so many of these tragedies."

"He is also suspected of dealing drugs."

"Herrera is an ordinary name."

Norah drew a five-by-six manila envelope from her handbag. It held a photograph, which she showed Judith Barthelmess.

"Yes, that's Mr. Herrera," she admitted. "Look, Lieutenant, when a client commits himself to the purchase of a three-million-dollar property and doesn't quibble about the financing, we don't investigate his background. We deal with a lot of foreigners: Orientals, Arabs, Latinos. They've all got money and they're all investing it in chunks of the United States: hotels, department stores, residences, airlines, television stations. You name it, they'll buy it. I had no reason to suspect Mr. Herrera was anything but one such businessman."

"No reason you should have," Norah agreed. "Let's get back to Randall Tye. When you told him the house he was interested in was sold, what was his reaction?"

"He wanted to make a counteroffer. I told him the house was no longer available. The closing had taken place. It didn't faze him. He offered to top whatever price the buyer had paid. 'A quick turnover,' he suggested."

"As you assumed Mr. Herrera was a legitimate businessman, wasn't that reasonable?"

"Yes, except that I couldn't understand why Mr. Tye was set on that particular property."

"Why should you care? It would have done no harm to relay Mr. Tye's offer," Norah suggested. "After all, the more times a property turns over, the more commissions there are for you. Isn't that right?"

"Certainly. And I did agree to transmit his offer."

"What happened?"

"Nothing happened, Lieutenant Mulcahaney. That was Friday late afternoon. This is Monday. I haven't got to it yet."

"I understand. You must be very busy with your husband's campaign and the primaries coming up."

"Yes."

"So that's the way it was left."

Judith Barthelmess nodded.

The chair Norah sat in was down-cushioned, ultracomfortable, but she couldn't relax. The room was cozy. The flowering branches of a magnolia tree filled the picture window, obscuring the street and the cars. The atmosphere was calm, but she wasn't reassured. Why had Randall come here? What had he been looking for? Had he found it? So far she hadn't asked the right questions.

"Mr. Tye hasn't been seen since he left here Friday afternoon. He's missed two of his regular telecasts. Are you aware of that?"

"No."

"Did he give you any indication of what he intended to do next? Where he was going?"

"I'm sorry."

"Please think hard, Mrs. Barthelmess. Randall Tye is a responsible person. It's not like him to just walk away without letting anyone know what he's up to. He's never missed a show. I'm worried about him."

Up to now Norah's reaction to Randall's behavior had been irritation. With those words she acknowledged anxiety. It wasn't a game between them anymore. Something had happened to Randall. Something bad.

Judith Barthelmess insisted on calling a cab for Lieutenant Mulcahaney and on keeping her company till it arrived. Both women were relieved when it arrived and they were finally able to say goodbye. Mrs. Barthelmess immediately returned to her office and called New York.

Impatiently she counted the rings, hoping he would pick up before the answering machine cut in; she didn't want to leave a message. And then, just as she was about to hang up, Ralph Dreeben came on.

"I thought you were going to take care of it," she snapped.

"Who's this? Judith? Take care of what?" the chairman asked mildly, covering his irritation.

"You know. Randall Tye."

"I told you not to worry about it."

"I had a woman here from the New York Police Department just now. Lieutenant Mulcahaney. She's Tye's girlfriend and she's smart."

"So?"

"Once Tye tells her . . ."

"What? What is he going to tell her? First, he doesn't know anything. Second, there's nothing to tell. How many times do I have to explain to you that you're in the clear? You're conducting a legitimate business. You're selling real estate and collecting a commission. There's nothing wrong with that. You're not required to investigate the seller or the buyer."

"I don't like it," she muttered.

"You can stop anytime," Ralph Dreeben reminded her. Then he turned soothing. "Up to now the operation has gone without a hitch to our mutual advantage. You don't think I'm going to allow a snooping reporter to throw a spanner into it? Or a female cop? Come on, Judith, you know better."

She sighed. "As long as Will doesn't find out. If Will ever finds out . . ."

"He won't. I promise. Okay?" Dreeben waited for an answer. "Okay, Judith?"

Norah didn't wait to get back to New York before putting out an APB, All Points Bulletin, for Randall Tye. She instructed the cab driver to pull over at the nearest telephone and contacted Ferdi Arenas. She also instructed Ferdi to go over to Randall Tye's apartment. If no one answered his ring, he was to get the manager to let him in. Then she got back in the cab and headed for the airport. She was back at the squad by six. Passing through to her office, she waved for Wyler and Ochs to follow.

"I want to know everything about Executive Transfers," she told Wyler. "If it's a private company, I want to know who owns it, who runs it, who works there. If it's public, I want to know who's on the board of directors." She turned to Ochs. "Get a list of the branches, the personnel in each branch and a client list, with particular attention to Washington, D.C., New York City, and suburbs. I'm particularly interested in repeat business."

"Suppose they don't want to cooperate?" Wyler asked.

She fixed him with a steady look. "Make them want to."

"Yes, ma'am."

"Just what are we looking for?" Ochs wanted to know.

Norah was silent for a while. "I'm not sure. I'm almost afraid to guess."

Getting access to records was one thing, Norah thought, analyzing them was something else. Not that she didn't have confidence in Wyler and Ochs; Ochs was particularly adept at this kind of thing, but an extra pair of eyes wouldn't hurt, particularly when they belonged to a real expert in bookkeeping. Norah put in a call to her old friend Gus Schmidt.

Chapter THIRTEEN

With the building manager a watchful presence, Fernando Arenas went through the Tye apartment. Unfortunately, a maid came in every day so the place was in perfect order. After an examination of the custom-designed closet with its rows of suits, shoes, drawer of shirts, sweaters, and so on, Ferdi could not conclude whether anything was missing. Brian Taft, the manager, informed Sergeant Arenas that Mr. Tye, along with most of the tenants, kept his luggage down in the basement trunk room and called whenever he required it. Mr. Tye had not done so in some time.

Ferdi phoned in.

So, Norah thought, Randall had gone to Washington specifically to talk to Judith Barthelmess and had intended to return the same day. But had he returned? Shuttle flights did not keep seat-reservation lists, but Randall was a celebrity and he might well have been noticed at the loading gate or by the cabin crew. She sent Ferdi out to LaGuardia.

She sent Nick Tedesco to check with the limo company. "Find out whether Randall ordered a car to meet him."

He hadn't. He hadn't called for a car on his return, either. Norah couldn't see Tye using public transportation, but Tedesco was instructed to check the airport taxi dispatcher anyway.

He came up empty on that, too. "Maybe he drove out?"

Although Randall Tye preferred the chauffeured limousine provided by the network and didn't particularly enjoy driving himself, he did own a Mercedes, which he kept in the building garage.

Norah contacted the parking attendant herself and was informed the car was gone. According to the time sheet, Mr. Tye had picked it up at noon on Friday and returned at nine-fourteen that night. He took it out again at eleven the next morning, and the car had not been seen since.

He might have gone back to Washington, Norah thought, or Puerto Rico and put the car in the long-term parking lot at one of the airports. With the help of airport security at Kennedy, LaGuardia, and Newark, the various lots, including metered parking areas, were checked. It took until nearly eleven P.M. for the results to come in. Randall Tye's Mercedes was not within the confines of those three airports.

Where in hell was it?

Norah was both worried and exasperated. Randall would have driven himself only if he didn't want anybody to know where he was going. She put out another APB, this time on the car. Then, tired and more worried than she cared to admit, she went home. Her last thought as she put out the light was: *Where was Randall?*

According to the digital display of her clock radio she was awakened at precisely two-ten A.M., and she knew instinctively as she reached for the telephone that it was not going to be good news.

"It's Ferdi, Norah. We've found him."

Despair enveloped her. She knew what was coming.

"In his car," Ferdi said. "Off the shoulder of the Grand Central Parkway on the far side of the old Aquacade."

Knowing there was no hope, she nevertheless had a surge of hope. "An accident?"

"No. He seems to have pulled over voluntarily. A bunch of kids spotted the car. They were getting ready to strip it. . . . I'm sorry, Norah."

She nearly missed it. The Grand Central Parkway, usually clogged with traffic, was just about deserted and invited speed. Though she had been given its approximate location and was on the lookout for the car, it was so well hidden behind a planting of Japanese pines that she would have gone right by if not for the police searchlights. Seeing them, she braked, skidded onto the grass verge, then bumped along to where a cluster of men stood silhouetted in the light of the full moon high in the sky and its reflection off the waters of the bay.

The usual investigative contingent was already there: a couple of traffic patrol cars, at least four RMPs, unmarked cars probably belonging to Queens detectives. The morgue wagon had arrived also, and Norah recognized Phil Worgan's car. He came from a greater distance than she and to have arrived ahead of her, Ferdi must have notified him right away, even before her. He would do that for only one reason—it was going to be very bad. She lined up her car with the others, turned off the ignition and lights, and started for the beige Mercedes which was the focus of all attention, but Ferdi stepped in her way.

"What've we got?" she asked automatically. In the one brief glance, she had discerned no damage. Only the fact that both doors were wide open suggested anything might be out of the ordinary.

Ferdi swallowed nervously; he looked sallow in the moonlight. He had gone over and over in his mind how best to put it and had decided there was only one way—say it straight out. "It looks like an OD."

"What?"

"I'm sorry, Norah."

She thought she was prepared for anything; she thought her past experience inured her to surprise. "No. No. It's not possible."

Ferdi was miserable. "There's not a scratch on the car, and there's no indication of violence on . . . the victim." He winced and hurried on. "It looks like he felt himself drifting off so he pulled over and then . . ."

"And then what, Sergeant?" Norah's blue eyes bored into those of Fernando Arenas, her old friend.

"And then he died."

"That's it? There could have been all kinds of reasons for him to pull over: he thought something was wrong with the car; he felt sleepy; he'd had too much to drink. Why should it have been drugs?"

Ferdi could hardly bear to look at her, but he couldn't say the words and not face her. "For one thing, the way the car is hidden suggests he didn't want anybody to see . . ." He paused, then blurted out, "There are tracks. Needle tracks."

Norah's gaze never wavered. "Get out of my way."

Phillip Worgan was the next obstacle.

"I want you to give it to me straight, Phil. Don't try to protect me. What happened?"

"There's every indication that he OD'd."

"No. It's not possible," she reiterated doggedly. "Randall didn't do drugs."

"See for yourself." Worgan stepped to one side and, at his signal, so did the orderlies who had been about to prepare Randall Tye for transport. The RMP cops and the detectives opened a path for Norah.

The smell of death warned her. It told her what to expect. She had known, of course, as soon as she saw the car why both doors were wide open and she had been subconsciously steeling herself for this moment, for what she would see. Nevertheless, it took every effort of her will to look inside. Randall sat behind the wheel, his head tilted back against the headrest, his amber eyes closed. The process of decay had begun.

She turned away, having already seen too much.

The realization that Randall was lost to her forever swept over her with a palpable, stabbing pain. Norah had stood in the presence of untimely and violent death many times—it was part of her job—but only once before had she been confronted by it in the person of someone she loved. The desolation she'd felt upon the death of her husband overwhelmed her now. He had been killed four years and four months ago, and though the sharpness of her sorrow had abated, it would never disappear completely.

Norah could still recall what Joe had looked like on the slab in the morgue. And now she would remember Randall. She closed her eyes and said a silent prayer. She asked God for the repose of Randall's soul. She asked for help in finding his killer. Then, opening her eyes, she looked once again, but not at his face.

He was wearing a light-gray tweed suit, jacket off and folded neatly on the seat beside him. White shirt, somewhat soiled, collar open and tie loosed. French cuffs held in place by jade cuff links. The left cuff was open and the sleeve rolled back above his elbow. Despite the green-blue discoloration of the veins indicating that he had been dead at least twenty-four hours, needle tracks were discernible.

"Was his sleeve rolled up like this when you found him?" she asked Ferdi.

Worgan answered for him. "No. He was wearing the jacket. I took it off him and then rolled up his sleeve."

"Why?"

Worgan's answer was to point to the hypodermic needle on the dashboard ledge.

Norah bit her lip. "Did you examine him for other marks or bruises —bullet wounds, cuts, slashes? He could have been poisoned."

"This isn't the place," Worgan chided her gently. "We'll look for any and all of those when we get him on the table. He was an important man, Norah, in a stressful profession. A lot of people in the media and in the show business do drugs."

"You stick to medicine, Doctor. I'll do the investigating."

"Sorry."

"No, no, I'm sorry, Phil. I apologize, but you didn't know Randall Tye. You have no reason to doubt what you see, no reason to look for any other cause of death. I do. He was a decent and dedicated man. I am not going to let him die in shame." Her voice broke. The tears coursed down her cheeks and she let them.

Ferdi had never seen her cry openly like this. Never. Instinctively, he started toward her but a look from Worgan warned him. After a while, Norah took out a handkerchief and wiped her face.

"When do you estimate death occurred?" she asked the medical examiner.

"Some time around midnight on Saturday," he replied. He wished he could be more specific. Knowing that Tye was lying out here all that time with cars speeding by, that someone might have found him and possibly saved him would only add to her anguish.

Clenching her fists and thrusting her chin forward, she asked Ferdi, "Was there a parking ticket?"

"Not on him."

"How about the glove compartment? Randall put in a hefty expense account, but he documented every item."

Before she could move, Arenas went around to the passenger side of the Mercedes—no way he was going to let Norah do it—and opened the glove compartment. He brought out a wad of receipts and memos and handed them to her.

Sorting through, she found what she wanted. "Here. He drove *In* to the lot at one-thirty P.M. Friday and *Out* at seven-forty-four P.M. Wait, there's another one. It's marked *In* at eight-twenty P.M. Saturday and *Out* at ten P.M. Saturday." She paused. "I spoke to him Friday morning. Apparently, he picked up his car shortly after, flew to Washington and returned that evening. He parked in the building garage and went out again Saturday morning. According to these tickets, he didn't go out to the airport till Saturday night. And he didn't take a plane anywhere. So why did he go?"

No one offered an opinion.

"He didn't stay in the lot very long," Worgan pointed out.

"You think he came out to the airport to meet his connection? You think he made his buy and couldn't wait to shoot up?" Norah challenged.

Worgan sighed.

"Then how come the car isn't headed back toward the city? How come it's pointed towards LaGuardia?"

Worgan could only shake his head.

"It doesn't play," Norah said and she was very positive. "No way. He would have had to be really desperate to shoot up in the car. But if he'd been injected against his will . . ."

"There's no indication of a struggle."

"He could have been sedated."

"You don't give up, do you?"

"Just take another look at his arm, Phil," Norah urged. "Look at those tracks. Go ahead."

"Well . . ."

"Stop being embarrassed for me. Forget about my feelings. Don't you notice anything?"

Worgan frowned. "The tracks are all fresh." His brow cleared. "They were all made at the same time."

"Exactly. Do me a favor, Phil. Don't let on there's any question about the OD as cause of death. Let whoever rigged this think we buy it."

Worgan looked at Norah with undisguised admiration. "I'll tell you one thing—if I ever get into a tight spot, I want you on my side."

Chapter

FOURTEEN

Norah got no more sleep that night. She knew that allowing the killer to think the police believed Randall had died of a drug overdose also meant destroying Randall's reputation. Norah could imagine what the public reaction would be. All his faults would be magnified. His indiscretions would be sought out and slavered over. Those who had most admired him would most vilify him. Norah's every instinct cried out to protect him, but she had no choice, not if she wanted to catch his killer.

Ferdi had offered to stay with her for the rest of the night. Then he suggested she might like Concepción to come over. She turned both offers down. She needed to be alone, to grieve and also to think. Drinking coffee and pacing through the lonely hours till dawn and then sunrise, Norah was dismayed to realize how little she'd actually known about the man who had become so very important to her and about whom she'd cared deeply. She knew about his professional history, everybody did, but almost nothing about his private life. She knew he had been married twice before, but to whom and why the marriages had failed, Randall had never said and she hadn't asked.

Her alarm went off at six-forty-five as usual. She took a shower, changed her clothes, and had another cup of coffee while she listened to the radio. The news of Randall Tye's death was all over the dial. What surprised Norah was the reaction of his colleagues. They were compassionate. Shock was everywhere apparent, yet they took the drug aspect in stride. For every public figure in entertainment, sports, communications, politics, and crime, there was a file in every media morgue. So there was for Randall Tye. A résumé of his life was instantly available and the commentators were able to add their personal slant for color.

Randall, Norah learned, had in fact a history of morphine involvement. It had been administered to him over a period of months while he lay in the hospital recovering from a botched operation on his right leg. Due to an infection, he had come close to having the leg amputated. Further surgery had proved successful, but left him with a slight, almost imperceptible limp.

Randall had explained the limp as the result of a war wound, but he hadn't mentioned anything about bungled surgery nor a temporary dependence on morphine to Norah.

In their professional research into their colleague's past, the media was already in possession of facts Norah hadn't known, saving both her and the squad numberless man hours. However, the press could not do more than speculate on what had turned Randall Tye back to drugs after successfully breaking his addiction. They cited the stress of the job, knowing it only too well themselves, and noted that Tye had recently taken on additional responsibilities as top anchor at Liberty Network. Along with his *People in the News* show and the regular six o'clock newscasts, Tye was preparing a new weekly program, a two-hour, in-depth coverage of a top news event. Sources also revealed he was conducting a personal investigation of the flea-market shooting and was on the verge of a big break.

Nor were Tye's personal affairs exempt from examination. He was presently unattached after having been twice married and divorced. It was rumored his private life had hit a snag.

Norah snapped off the radio.

She had actually left the building before she realized it was raining, and she had to go back up for a raincoat and an umbrella. Then she decided it wasn't coming down hard enough to warrant taking the car. Actually, it was gentle, little more than a soothing mist, she thought as she started across town to the station house. She entered the park at Sixty-eighth Street. The grass was fresh, the bright green of spring, the trees lining the Mall formed a translucent canopy. She slowed her pace and stopped trying to force the jumble of facts into a pattern. She let her mind relax. Descending the broad flight of shallow steps that led to the Bethesda Fountain, she followed the curving path along the lake to the Bow Bridge and crossed over to her favorite spot—a bench just at the edge of The Ramble.

She was committed to the belief that Randall's death had not been suicide, nor accident, but murder. The next question was—why? In his position, Randall probably had enemies he didn't even know about, so for the moment she would set motive aside and consider the MO. Why had drugs been chosen as the instrument of death? It stipulated that the perpetrator had easy access to drugs, but nowadays that didn't much narrow the field. Drugs could have been chosen to camouflage murder because it was easier than rigging an accident—a car crash, say, or a fall from a high place, or food poisoning. But it didn't feel right. In choosing to use drugs, the perp had shown a knowledge of Randall's past which, close as she'd been to him, even Norah hadn't been aware of.

Despite their clashes, Norah and Randall had a lot in common including a good sense of humor. He had introduced Norah to his celebrity friends, urging her not to be in awe of them. To that end, he'd told her stories that brought the rock stars, bestselling authors, champion athletes, down to the common level and they'd laughed together. Norah had responded with stories about herself, and she realized now that Randall had avoided talking about himself except where it involved the future. She had told him everything, but he had not trusted her with his past. It added to the hurt.

Norah got up and continued on her usual route to the Seventy-ninth Street exit at Central Park West. But having reached it, she went on.

Why had Randall been killed at this particular time? He'd told her he was on the verge of a big break in the flea-market shooting. He'd expected to have the solution within forty-eight hours, but within forty-eight hours, he was dead.

It was well after nine when Norah walked into the squad room. Art Potts grabbed her.

"The C of D wants you."

"Oh?"

"Forthwith."

"Oh." That meant urgent, right away, yesterday. Norah's eyebrows went up, but she didn't get overly excited. "Anything else?"

"Isn't that enough?"

"You know what I mean. Anything from Schmidt?"

"He's digging. They're all digging."

"In that case, I'd better find out what the Chief wants."

She took the subway down to One Police Plaza. Despite the constant delays, breakdowns, and other interruptions of service, it was still the quickest way to get around the city. Norah presented herself to Chief Deland's secretary.

"The meeting's just breaking up," Officer Gilda Kamenar chided, while at the same time buzzing her boss's office. "Go right in," she told Norah.

Jim Felix was there. Norah wasn't surprised. At the rank of Inspector, he had served as Chief Deland's executive officer. Now, despite promotion to three-star chief and the added responsibilities, Deland still relied on him and consulted with him. There was only one other person present, a man she had never met but recognized before they were introduced—Ralph Dreeben, local politician, party boss on the verge of retirement or maybe already retired—Norah wasn't sure.

Dreeben held out his hand and beamed.

Norah was instinctively wary of the charm exuded by public figures. One of the tests of sincerity was eye contact. Did the celebrity bother to really look at the lesser person? Dreeben passed that test and the next— he got her name right.

"So, you're Lieutenant Mulcahaney. I've heard a lot about you. All of it good."

"Thank you, sir."

Chief Deland waved her to a chair. She took it and waited. She didn't ask what Dreeben was doing there. It wasn't her place to do so and she'd find out soon enough, she thought. And she did, but it wasn't anything she could have guessed or prepared for.

"I'm only sorry we're meeting on such an occasion," Dreeben continued.

Instinctively, Norah looked to Jim Felix.

"I'm sorry to add to your troubles."

"We know that you and Randall Tye were very close," Felix explained.

"Perhaps this should wait for another time?" Dreeben suggested.

"No," Norah replied. "Whatever it is, I'd like to know about it now."

Dreeben opened both hands in a gesture of acquiescence.

"You went to Washington, D.C., yesterday to see Judith Barthelmess," Felix stated. "For what purpose?"

Norah understood he was laying a foundation for Chief Deland. "I was trying to locate Randall Tye. He'd been missing for two days and that was the last place he was known to have been and Mrs. Barthelmess was the last person known to have spoken with him."

"Are you implying that Mrs. Barthelmess was in some way involved with Mr. Tye's disappearance?" Dreeben asked, still genial.

"No, sir, that was not my intention," Norah replied. "Mrs. Barthelmess told me Randall wanted to buy a certain house on Long Island but that it was already sold."

"What was wrong with that?"

"Nothing. Not insofar as I know," Norah qualified. "I questioned Mrs. Barthelmess about her handling the property. It was my understanding that real-estate agencies operated on a local level. She explained to me the rather special service provided by her company, Executive Transfers."

"She says you didn't accept the explanation and continued to harass her."

"I was worried about Randall, but I certainly didn't intend to cause Mrs. Barthelmess distress. If I did, I apologize. Please tell her so."

Dreeben's eyes bored into her.

"Under the circumstances, I certainly won't be bothering her anymore," Norah added.

Evidently, that was what Dreeben wanted to hear. He rose and extended his hand. "Again, Lieutenant, my condolences." He shook hands with the two chiefs and was gone.

Norah could hardly wait till the door closed behind him. "I did not harass Mrs. Barthelmess." Her blue eyes blazed, her chin jutted out. "I questioned her about her dealings with Juan Herrera. She explained them logically and I had to accept what she said. I assume she also satisfied Randall, although now . . . I'm not so sure. His death is convenient, don't you think?"

"Not necessarily," Deland replied, discarding the unlit cigar he had been chewing on throughout the interview.

"He was investigating Juan Herrera's drug connection and it led him to Judith Barthelmess and now to Ralph Dreeben."

Deland selected a fresh cigar and settled it comfortably at the side of his mouth. "Let's not get carried away."

"Randall got hooked through no fault of his own," Norah went on. "But he kicked the habit and he's been clean for years. Why should he suddenly start up again?"

"Personal disappointment?" Felix looked at her.

Norah flushed. "There was nothing settled between us—one way or another. No, it's a setup. Randall was a first-class investigative reporter.

He turned up a lead and he was killed to keep his mouth shut. What's more, he was killed by someone from his past."

Deland cast a look at Felix. "You're emotionally involved, Lieutenant. I think it would be better if somebody took over from here on."

"No, sir!"

A warning flashed from Jim Felix's green eyes, but Norah ignored it. "I'm not going to withdraw voluntarily, Chief. I did that once before and the case was never cleared." Felix passed a hand over his brow; Deland chomped down hard on the cigar and his temples pulsed: both knew she referred to the murder of her husband. "I'm not saying I would have made a difference then, but I should have tried. You'll have to kick me off this time." She squared her shoulders and looked straight at the chief.

"Then I suppose you'd snoop around on your own," Deland remarked mildly.

Too mildly? Norah wondered. Had she gone too far? She didn't care. She meant what she'd said. "I would."

"How many times have you stood in front of this desk, Lieutenant, and challenged me?"

"Sir, it's not a challenge. It's a request. No, a plea. Let me continue on the case. I think Randall was on to something really big. I think I'm the one who can best follow his tracks."

The chief continued to chew on his unlit cigar. "All right," he decided. "But stay away from Mrs. Barthelmess and from Ralph Dreeben. That's an order. If you get to the point where you can't proceed without making contact with one or the other, clear it with Chief Felix. In fact, you report to Chief Felix on every new line of investigation. We could get into real big trouble on this one. The three of us. Understood?"

"Yes, sir. Understood."

"And one more thing, Lieutenant."

"Sir?"

"I suggest you don't disabuse the press and public of the notion that Randall Tye died of an accidental OD. I know you're anxious to clear his name. I think for the time being, however, you should let the assumption stand."

"Yes sir, I agree."

"Do you? That's good, Lieutenant." Deland rose, went over to her, and took both her hands in his. "I am sorry, Norah. He was a good man."

The tears sprang to Norah's eyes. She nodded, and walked out quickly.

Work was the best cure for grief and no one knew that better than Norah. With Joe's death, she had lost a part of her life. This was not the same. There had been no actual commitment between her and Randall. She had lost what might have been. The killer had robbed her of the future. Now, because of orders, she was left floundering without a clear line of investigation to follow. On the way to the subway, she noticed a street phone and on a hunch stopped to dial the ME's private line.

"It's Norah, Phil. Have you got anything for me?"

"Give me a break; it's only been a few hours." Worgan offered the usual excuse. But knowing the strain she was under, immediately changed attitude. "I'm not finished, but I can tell you that the death was in fact due to an overdose of heroin. I can't give you the exact amount, but I don't suppose you care. He had also ingested Seconal. I don't have the figures on that either, but it was enough to knock him out."

"I knew it. I knew it." Norah sighed softly. "The killer slipped him the Seconal and then injected him when he passed out."

"Could very well be."

"Why should he take Seconal if he intended to shoot up?" Norah demanded. "Unless . . . is this some new synergistic combination?"

"If it is, I haven't heard about it," Worgan replied. "Personally, I think it happened the way you say. Officially . . ."

"That's okay. I'm satisfied. Thanks, Phil."

She hung up, satisfied that she'd been right. So now she was in possession of two strong leads: one, that the killer was someone familiar with Randall's past; two, that Randall had been comfortable enough with his killer to have a drink with him—coffee, a cocktail, whatever. She ran down the subway steps, caught the A train just as it was coming into the station, and rode back uptown to her office.

Gus Schmidt was waiting for her.

Seeing him brought a flood of memories. She particularly remembered Gus's kindness at the time of Joe's death. Norah had desperately needed to get away, and he had given her the use of a house he had inherited in the Amish country of Pennsylvania. Once again, she needed his help. She had called and though he was retired, he had instantly placed himself at her disposal.

Norah held out her arms and embraced him. Like Ferdi Arenas, the old sergeant was a stickler for decorum, but the warmth of Norah's greeting, the genuine spontaneity, cut through his reserve.

"It's so good to see you, Gus."

"Likewise."

"I appreciate your helping me out. I hope I'm not disrupting any private plans?"

"I wish you were. No, I have no plans. I'm glad you called."

At the end of his career, when he was getting too old to take pursuit, slow on the draw and way off the target, Norah had noted his thoroughness in research, his attention to detail, and suggested he take a course in bookkeeping. Schmidt had followed her advice and become an expert examiner and analyst of financial structure. He was thorough, perceptive, and fast. He wouldn't be here now unless he was on to something.

"What've you got for me, Gus?" Norah asked, as she went around to her chair and he pulled his closer to her desk.

"The information you wanted on Executive Transfers. I think you'll find it very interesting." He drew a sheaf of papers from a briefcase and placed it before her. "You'll notice more than one familiar name."

The top page listed transactions for the past six months. It gave a description of the properties and the names of the clients, both sellers and buyers. Norah ran her eye over it. There was Juan Herrera, as expected. There was also Bruno Branzini and Manolo Torres, both known druglords.

"How did you get this?"

Schmidt frowned. "Consider it information, not evidence."

That meant he had not got it legally. Norah was saddened. Never, in the years she had known Gus, had he ever departed from procedure as laid down in the Patrol Guide and the Detective Guide, much less performed an illegal act.

He knew what she was thinking; his gray eyes behind the thick, rimless glasses indicated it. "Times have changed, Norah. We can't play by the old rules. Not if we want to get the job done."

She had expected that Gus would be one of the last holdouts for the system. When a man like him lost faith, they were in real trouble, she thought but didn't say any more.

And Gus Schmidt, taking her silence as tacit approval of his illegal entry into the New York offices of Executive Transfers, reached across and turned the page. "You'll notice that Mrs. Barthelmess handled both purchases and sales for Herrera, Branzini, and Torres. You'll also notice that million-dollar properties were being turned over with little profit—except for the agent."

"Mrs. Barthelmess."

"Exactly."

It was a simple and effective money-laundering scheme, Norah thought: dirty money going in to buy a house and coming out clean when the house was sold. Drugs directly linked to Mrs. Barthelmess's real-estate operation. She was shocked that a woman of Judith Barthelmess's class and background would lend herself to it. Unless, of course, she didn't know what was going on. But how could she not know? She had protested to Norah that she didn't ask a man with a couple of million dollars on the table where he got his money. Okay, insofar as the client was an unknown quantity. Maybe you could argue that Herrera was not big enough to be generally recognized as a druglord, but you couldn't say that about Branzini and Torres. They were notorious.

No wonder Randall had been excited, Norah thought. No wonder he'd played his cards close to his chest. The charges he would be making required absolute verification. He was about to accuse the wife of a congressman and candidate for the U.S. Senate of doing business with druglords. Inevitably, suspicion would fall on Will Barthelmess as well. Randall couldn't go on the air without absolute proof of his allegations, but before he could get it, he was killed.

If only he'd shared his suspicions, Norah agonized. Maybe he'd been afraid that she would be obliged to inform her superior, Manny Jacoby. The captain would in turn have to go to his boss and the chain would lead all the way to the top. She recalled the last time they'd talked. Randall had been on the verge of disclosing what he suspected; she'd sensed it. Then he'd changed his mind and asked for that final, fatal forty-eight hours.

"The last person we know saw Randall alive was Judith Barthelmess," Norah told Gus. "He went to see her ostensibly to buy a house. He said he was thinking about getting married." Her voice quavered; she swallowed and went on. "I don't imagine she believed him. A couple of days later I went to Washington and interrogated Mrs. Barthelmess. Apparently, that added to her nervousness and she appealed to Ralph Dreeben. He went to Chief Deland and now I've been ordered to stay clear of both of them."

"This might get the Chief to change his mind," Gus replied and placed one more sheet in front of Norah. "This is a list of the officers of Executive Transfers."

The name jumped out at Norah. It was the second from the top: Ralph Dreeben, Vice President.

Chapter
FIFTEEN

Norah went first to Captain Jacoby as Randall had known she would. Jacoby in turn was obliged to go higher. The buck stopped at Jim Felix's desk. It was his job to protect Chief Deland as it was Deland's to run interference for the PC.

"This doesn't necessarily mean that Dreeben had knowledge of the money-laundering scheme, much less that he was personally involved in it or in Randall's death," Felix pointed out to Jacoby and to Norah. "Judith Barthelmess could have appealed to him because as a local politician of prominence and an officer of the company, he was the one most likely to be able to help her."

The rain had stopped, and the rays of the setting sun breaking through the clouds tinted the walls of the Bureau Chief's office.

"That would be stretching coincidence," Norah protested.

"Better than making an unfounded accusation." As ever, Jacoby was overly cautious. "We're dealing with a man's honor and reputation."

"How about Randall's honor and reputation?" Norah demanded. "Who's going to defend that? How about his life? Who's going to give that back to him?"

Felix put up a hand to silence them both. "What we've got to be concerned about is the extent of this thing. It's known that Mrs. Barthelmess is using her own money to help finance her husband's campaign. Apparently, the money is coming from illegal transactions. We have to ask ourselves—does Will Barthelmess know the money is tainted? Does he know and condone it? Could he be involved in the scam? Once the facts are public there's bound to be a strong suspicion of guilt. True or false, he's not likely to survive in politics."

Norah frowned. "That's too bad. If he's innocent, I'm sorry for him, but . . ."

"Could it be why Randall Tye was being so secretive?" Felix interrupted. "Maybe he wasn't sure of Barthelmess's position. Maybe he didn't want to destroy the career of an innocent man. I think we should respect that."

"All right. Yes." Norah bit her lip to hold back tears. She was grateful for Felix's tribute. "But Randall is dead, so now we have no choice but to turn over every stone and look under every clod."

"All right," Felix nodded. "But no leak in regard to the money laundering. What we're discussing is not to go beyond the three of us here."

"Gus Schmidt already knows. He's the one who uncovered the scheme," Norah pointed out.

"Gus will keep his mouth shut," Felix said.

"So will my team."

"No. I don't want you to tell them."

"I can't send people out without telling them what they're after," she protested. "They won't know what to look for or what questions to ask."

"The Chief ordered hands off Dreeben and Mrs. Barthelmess," Felix reminded her.

"The situation has changed."

Felix shook his head.

"All right, I'll work alone."

"I'm not crazy about that."

"I'll let them know that I'm working unofficially because of my personal feelings for Randall. They know I cared for him so they'll buy it," Norah argued. "If they don't, if it all goes bad, you can always say I acted against orders."

Felix scowled. He looked to Manny Jacoby, who up to this point had stayed out of it. Jacoby's round face oozed sweat.

"Nobody in my command disobeys orders."

"Good." Felix turned back to Norah. "Do what you have to do. We'll back you."

The rain had started early that morning and was predicted to last into tomorrow, but as Manny Jacoby and Norah came out of the Big Building, there was a temporary break. Jacoby offered her a ride back to the precinct, but she declined. She had a couple of errands en route, she said.

His small eyes fixed on her. "You call on me if you need anything. People who traffic in drugs don't deserve any consideration."

She was both surprised and grateful and didn't know how to say so. She nodded, and watched as he got into the car and drove off.

How many times had Randall Tye insisted his job and hers were alike, that they followed the same routines? Police officers kept notes; they were required to. So did investigative reporters. There had been no notes on Randall's person, not even an address book. The killer undoubtedly had searched and taken away anything that might incriminate him. But suppose Randall didn't have anything on him?

He did a lot of work at home, just as she did, so there was the possibility that he might have his notes or even a rough draft of a script there. But Ferdi had gone through the apartment. Could he have overlooked something like that? Not likely, Norah thought, but worth her going to take another look. Was it possible Randall would keep that kind of information in his office? She called in and told Simon Wyler to go over to the Liberty Network, then she took the subway uptown and walked the few short blocks to Randall's building. The manager accompanied her as he had Ferdi Arenas, put the key in the lock, turned the knob and opened the door.

He stopped on the threshold.

The place had been ransacked; drawers emptied, their contents in piles on the floor; books taken down from the shelves, spines bent back. The sofa and chairs had their pillows pulled out and cut open. The pictures taken off the walls had their backs ripped.

Brian Taft gasped. "I was in here yesterday with Sergeant Arenas and everything was fine. I don't understand."

Norah was already on the phone to notify the burglary squad. They would bring in photographers, fingerprint experts, locksmiths, etc. No need for her to wait around; any documentation Randall might have had was gone.

"I don't understand," Taft repeated. "I don't understand how this could have happened. We're very security-conscious in this building."

What Norah didn't understand was the time lapse. Shouldn't the search have been made immediately after the murder? It seemed almost like an afterthought.

* * *

As predicted, it was still raining the next morning, so Norah took the car and drove out to Queens. She parked in the lot adjacent to the Borough Hall, crossed Queens Boulevard, and, hunching under the umbrella that was almost useless in the wind, walked two blocks up toward the Maple Grove Cemetery to Ralph Dreeben's office.

His reception room was crowded. Though he was on the verge of withdrawing as party chairman, the aging politician was still a leader and hero to the people of the borough. They still came to him with their problems and he made every effort to serve them. The quarters he inhabited were functional, purposely ordinary, the intent being to reassure rather than impress. The people of Queens owed Ralph Dreeben a lot and would support him against almost any charge. Both Norah Mulcahaney and the retiring boss knew that.

"You want my alibi for the night Randall Tye died of an overdose of heroin, Lieutenant?" he asked and managed to sound both amused and sympathetic at the same time. "I was attending a dinner in my honor at the Terrace in the Sky restaurant."

Interestingly, it was located on the site of the old World's Fair and close to LaGuardia airport and the place Randall and his car had been found.

"It started at seven-thirty with cocktails and broke up shortly after eleven."

"And then?"

"I was given to understand that Mr. Tye died between ten-thirty P.M. and midnight."

That had not been made public, so he was letting her know he had private sources. She, in turn, let him see she wasn't impressed. "That's a loose estimate, Mr. Dreeben. Once the autopsy is completed, the medical examiner may make it earlier or later. He'll certainly narrow it down."

"Afterwards, I went home to Jamaica Estates. My wife died recently, so I live alone. You can check with my chauffeur. You'll also discover that I don't drive, so once he delivered me to my own door, that was it."

"It seems conclusive," she said but gave no indication of leaving. Dreeben should be counterattacking, she thought. He should be asking, even demanding, why she wanted to know. "How long have you been on the board of Executive Transfers?" she asked bluntly and thought she detected, at last, a flicker of alarm.

"Two or three years. Why?"

"When Mrs. Barthelmess complained to you that I was harassing her, did she say in what way?"

"She said you called on her ostensibly to locate Randall Tye and wound up questioning certain business transactions."

"I believe that Randall uncovered a money-laundering scheme linked to Executive Transfers through Mrs. Barthelmess."

"I am a vice president of Executive Transfers, but I don't take part in day-to-day operations."

"In other words, you don't know what's going on."

"I know there's nothing going on that shouldn't be going on," he flared.

"Doesn't it seem odd to you that Mrs. Barthelmess is turning the same set of properties over and over?"

He shrugged. "Those particular properties are marketable, and she's an excellent saleswoman."

"Is that what you told Randall Tye?"

"I didn't speak to Mr. Tye. I told you where I was on the night . . ."

"I'm not referring to the night of his murder."

"Murder!"

"I believe he was murdered, yes." His sources hadn't told him that, Norah observed with satisfaction.

"Murder," Dreeben sighed.

"I'm talking about the night before; and the Saturday morning. He did come to see you, didn't he? Not here, of course, but at your home. I think he was concerned with how far the scheme had spread, who was involved. I think most of all he was concerned over how much Will Barthelmess knew or suspected. Barthelmess was the ultimate beneficiary, after all, wasn't he? His wife's commissions were, are, financing his campaign."

"I can't say, Lieutenant." Dreeben was grave. "It appears there may have been illegalities in the conduct of business at Executive Transfers that I knew nothing about. Perhaps you're right and Mrs. Barthelmess is using dirty money to finance her husband's race for the nomination, but I'm not aware of it and I doubt very much Will Barthelmess is. The man is a straight arrow, incorruptible. In fact, to be honest, Will Barthelmess's probity has been somewhat of a liability. He lost his first race because he wouldn't accept contributions with strings attached. He wanted to be his own man. As far as I know, he always has been.

During his term in the Congress, he's gained the reputation of resisting deals and trade-offs. Ethically, he's squeaky clean. If he so much as suspected his campaign funds were not coming from simon-pure sources, he wouldn't accept them. Rather than accept, he'd withdraw."

"That's quite a testimonial."

"Every word is true. You can be sure he doesn't know. His wife would see to it that he didn't find out."

Ah! Norah thought and caught her breath. Did Dreeben realize what he was implying? Of course, he was a shrewd politician, not likely to make unconsidered admissions, so she had to wonder if indeed he not only did realize, but had made the statement to direct Norah's attention.

Just how important was Barthelmess's election to the retiring political boss? Norah wondered. Dreeben was accustomed to working behind the scenes. As head of the party all kinds of jobs and contracts fell under his patronage. It gave him power. Soon he would be losing it, she thought. But with Barthelmess in the Senate and grateful to Dreeben for helping put him there, he could salvage considerable clout. Just how far was Dreeben prepared to go to ensure the attractive congressman's election?

How close were the ties between Dreeben and Judith Barthelmess? Evidently, not so close for he chose to sacrifice her in order to protect her husband.

By the time Norah left Dreeben's office, the rain had stopped and the sun broken through the clouds, but the humidity remained oppressive. Steam rose from the puddles in the parking lot. Impulsively, without really giving herself time to ponder, Norah headed not for her car but for a row of public telephones in front of the courthouse and put in a call to Judith Barthelmess's private line in Georgetown.

"Lieutenant Mulcahaney, Mrs. Barthelmess. I need to speak with you again."

"Yes, Lieutenant?"

"I mean in person. I could be there early this afternoon."

"Oh." An awkward pause. "I'm very sorry, but it's not convenient. I've told you everything I can."

"This is not about your real-estate business, Mrs. Barthelmess. When we spoke I thought Randall Tye was alive, but he wasn't. So I want to talk to you now about his death."

"I don't know anything about that, Lieutenant."

"I cared for Randall Tye," Norah said and paused and for the moment couldn't say any more.

"I realize that, Lieutenant and you have my sympathy, but I honestly don't know how I can help."

"Give me fifteen, twenty minutes of your time. I can get on the next shuttle. I'm halfway to the airport now."

"No," Judith Barthelmess broke in decisively. "No. I plan to be in New York tomorrow. I'll be staying at the Plaza. I could probably see you there at about three. Can it wait till then, Lieutenant Mulcahaney?"

"Yes, ma'am," Norah said. What else could she say? And then hung up. Maybe it was just as well. She had alerted Ralph Dreeben to the fact that Randall's death was now looked upon as a homicide. She had hinted as much to Mrs. Barthelmess. They had till three tomorrow afternoon to decide how to handle it.

Norah got her team together to brainstorm the possibilities. After that, they discussed countermeasure, and Norah made the assignments. Then she went home.

It wasn't till she'd closed the door behind her, hung up her coat, gone into the bedroom, and slipped out of her shoes, that she realized how tired she was. She'd hardly slept at all the night before, but that was nothing new and the adrenaline of investigation usually kept her going. This weariness she felt was based on depression, on the pain of loss. She missed Randall and she was going to miss him even more; she hadn't till this moment realized how much she'd relied on him. It was part of her self-imposed discipline to cook a proper meal and set a place for herself in the dining room. Tonight, she warmed a can of lentil soup, made toast, and ate at the kitchen table.

Back in the living room, she sought diversion by trying to catch up on her reading. Randall had made the cover of *Time*. Norah read the piece carefully, particularly the part dealing with his hospital stay. At ten, she got up, checked the lock on her front door, but left the chain off. She did not expect any entry attempt to be made there. The bedroom window overlooked a fire escape and would be more logical. She left it open just enough to provide circulation. At twenty after ten, she put out the light.

* * *

Nicholas Tedesco was posted at the west corner, shielded from the golden arc lights of Third Avenue by shrubbery in the front yard of a small, private townhouse. Danny Neel was at the north corner, seated in his car. Julius Ochs, in the tattered guise of the homeless, was stretched across a doorway at the east. Dom Shalette, a recent transfer to the squad, watched from the counter of an all-night coffee shop at the south. Their attention was on the small apartment house halfway up Sixty-eighth, their job to alert the men hiding inside, Wyler and Arenas, of any suspicious activity. There were only fifteen apartments, and all the tenants were either home or accounted for. The night wore on, but the men on the stakeout were patient. They were accustomed to the long, empty hours. They remained alert.

Midnight. One A.M. Two A.M. Each man, without communicating over the two-way radios, tensed. This was the time of greatest danger. In these last hours of deepest night, while the innocent slept, when the defenses of the city were down, this was when it would happen, if it happened at all. At some time in those hours each man raised his eyes to the building's darkened fifth floor, each with mixed feelings about what might lie ahead.

Just before three, a group of teenagers, seven or eight boys and girls, turned the corner of Lexington Avenue and made their way toward Third. They were laughing and shouting, playfully pummeling and pushing each other. Tedesco observed them as did the others, but he was the closest.

One of the girls was wailing that she had lost her key.

"God! My parents will kill me," she squealed, partly frightened, but also enjoying the predicament.

It could be a ruse, Tedesco thought. Ochs pulled himself to his feet and, clutching his rags, peered out of the doorway. They were under orders to take no action till the suspect was inside, not only inside the building but inside the apartment. Better alert Wyler and Arenas to what all the ruckus was about, Tedesco decided and spoke softly into his communicator. "A bunch of kids are in front of the building trying to . . ."

The explosion put an end to the message.

After a moment of shocked immobility, the detectives dashed from their posts into the street to look up.

The windows on the fifth floor were blown out. Curtains billowed. A flicker of flame caught and consumed them. After a few moments when the noise of the explosion died, the crackle of the fire could be plainly discerned. In the silent night it was loud as thunder.

Huddled in the middle of the street, the teenagers screamed. Lights came on in the burning building and on the block. Windows were thrown open. Shalette, in the coffee shop, got on the phone to the fire department which had a sub-station around the corner in the Hunter College garage while the other detectives converged on the building.

Inside, Wyler and Arenas were racing up the five flights. Using his key, Ferdi opened the apartment door and they entered.

"Lieutenant!"

The bedroom door was off its hinges. Smoke poured out, black, acrid, stinging eyes and throat. Using a handkerchief wasn't much protection, but they stumbled on.

The bed was smoldering.

"Norah?" Ferdi called out.

The bathroom door opened.

"There's an extinguisher in the kitchen, in the cabinet under the sink," Norah said. Her voice shook. Fanned by the gust of air coming through a broken window, the mattress burst into flame and the dummy lying there caught fire.

Wyler went for the extinguisher.

"Are you all right, Norah?" Ferdi scrutinized her anxiously in the fitful light. "What happened?"

"Time bomb," she answered. "I considered the possibility but didn't think we needed the bomb squad. I figured we'd find the device ourselves when we checked out the apartment." She shook her head. "He's smarter than I thought."

"And you're smarter than he thought," Ferdi pointed out. "You weren't in the bed."

Chapter

SIXTEEN

Though the room was a shambles, serious damage was relatively slight. Sally Felix, Jim Felix's wife, invited Norah to stay with them while repairs were being made. Signora Emilia, Joe's mother, and the various sisters invited her to stay with them. Norah thanked them all, but declined. There was a spare bedroom and she'd be all right in that. There was no way to keep the explosion a secret from the media, but she played it down. She made sure there was no hint that a trap had been set, no mention of a dummy in her bed. She had been very tired, Norah was quoted as saying, and she had fallen asleep in the living room in front of the television. Luck, she stressed, sheer luck.

Asked if she had any idea who might have planted the device, Norah had shrugged.

"In my line of work you make enemies. It comes with the territory."

At two-thirty the next afternoon, Norah left the squad and took the subway down to Columbus Circle. From there it was a short walk to the Plaza Hotel. The weather continued unseasonably hot and oppressively humid, but the tourists that thronged Central Park South didn't seem to mind. Their eagerness, enthusiasm, and open-mouthed wonder identified them. A half dozen horse-drawn hansom cabs were lined up at the curb awaiting passengers. The famous old hotel was resplendent in the refurbishing lavished on it by its new owners—gaudy, some thought, but impressive, Norah decided as she entered the lobby. A string quartet played for those lingering over lunch in the Palm Court. As she stepped toward a housephone, she spotted the woman she'd come to see.

"Mrs. Barthelmess?"

Making her way through the crowd, Judith Barthelmess appeared not to hear. She was wearing a light-blue suit of silk, the waist nipped and the shoulders well padded. It was big on her. She couldn't have lost all that much weight since Norah had seen her, but she certainly didn't look well.

"Mrs. Barthelmess!" Norah raised her voice.

"Lieutenant." Judith Barthelmess stopped and waited for Norah to reach her. "Are you all right? I read in the paper about . . . the accident."

"Thank you, I'm fine. Not a scratch on me."

"You're lucky."

"Yes," Norah agreed.

"I tried to get hold of you at your office, but you'd already left. Something has come up. I have one commitment and then I have to head right back for Washington. So I'm afraid we'll have to postpone our meeting. I'm very sorry, but . . ."

"Where are you headed now?" Norah asked.

"Up to the ABC studios to make a tape."

"Do you have a car waiting?"

"No, there's usually a taxi."

"Traffic is terrible at this hour. Why don't we walk? And we can talk at the same time." She placed her hand on Judith Barthelmess's elbow and gently steered her around to the side exit.

Dodging traffic, the two women scurried across the street to the park entrance immediately opposite and found themselves on a path that sloped down to the lake. The lake was well below street level and thus sheltered from wind and noise. The water was still, but the gray sky dulled what on a sunny day would have been a sharply edged reflection of trees and city skyline. In mutual, unspoken accord, the women slowed.

"I love the park when it's empty and quiet like this," Norah said. "I feel all my tensions ease."

"Yes," Judith Barthelmess agreed, but it wasn't true. She was tighter than ever.

And Norah knew it. "When I spoke to you in your office in Georgetown on Monday, I told you Randall Tye had disappeared and that I was worried about him. You assured me you didn't know his whereabouts and . . ."

"That was true."

"And I took you at your word. You said Randall came to you with the sole purpose of purchasing a particular property and that he didn't question your dealings with Juan Herrera, dealings which you again assured me were totally innocent on your part. I accepted that, too."

"But . . ."

"But the situation has changed. Randall is dead. The instrument of his death was heroin."

Judith Barthelmess stopped, looked squarely at Norah. "Self-administered."

Norah didn't dispute it. "The question is—where did he get the drug?"

"Please, Lieutenant, you can't be asking seriously! Anybody can get any drug anywhere anytime."

"I'm sure Mr. Herrera would supply you with whatever you might need."

"Are you implying that I use drugs? Or that I supplied poor Randall Tye?"

Norah flushed to hear Randall referred to like that.

"Before you carry this any farther, Lieutenant Mulcahaney, you should consider the laws of libel."

"You made a lot of money through your real-estate deals, Mrs. Barthelmess, dirty money. Some of it, most of it probably, is going into your husband's campaign. That's why Randall went to see you, not to buy a house but to get proof of your money-laundering operation. Of course, he also wanted to know whether your husband was aware of where his funding was coming from."

Judith Barthelmess's face hardened. She clamped her lips tight, glared at Norah, then with a toss of her head walked off. Norah let her get a few feet ahead before calling.

"Where are you going?"

She didn't even turn her head.

"There's nothing you can do and no one who can help you." Norah spoke in a quiet voice that nevertheless carried in the still air. But she didn't get any response this time, either. "If you have any idea about another try at getting rid of me, forget it."

That stopped her. "I had nothing to do with the bombing of your apartment."

"You can tell whoever did that getting rid of me will not solve this problem. As an investigative reporter, Randall Tye was playing a lone hand. Police detectives don't work like that. It's a team effort. Everybody has access to the same information. What I know, everybody else on the squad and my boss and his boss, all the way to the top, knows."

They looked deep into each other's eyes.

Up on the street the blare of horns, screech of brakes, doormen's whistles seemed remote. Nearby, in the sanctuary, birds chirped. On the lake, a lone boater dipped his oars into the placid water and that was the loudest sound of all.

Judith Barthelmess's eyes filled. "When you called yesterday, Lieutenant, you appealed to me on the basis of what Randall Tye meant to you. I'm appealing to you now because of what my husband means to me. I'll admit that I knew money was being laundered through my real-estate transactions. Of course I knew it was illegal, but I didn't see that it hurt anybody. I mean, once the drugs were sold the damage was done. Once the money was in the dealers' hands, they were going to find some way to . . ."

"To clean it up?"

Judith Barthelmess sighed. "I don't sell drugs. I don't use them."

That was an obvious reference to Randall, but Norah held herself in check.

"My husband is everything to me, Lieutenant. He's my life. We've been married eighteen years. We have no children, but we share his career. To paraphrase Patricia Nixon—I've been an unpaid volunteer for Will Barthelmess for eighteen years. Will is an honest man. Ask anybody in the Congress, ask anybody in politics, and they'll tell you he's too honest for his own good. That's what's been holding him back.

"I want to see him get the Party's nomination and I want to see him elected. I think he has a lot to offer the country. I believe he can go higher than the Senate. I swear to you he doesn't know, doesn't have any suspicion of what's been going on and where his funding is coming from. He wouldn't tolerate it for one second. If he ever found out, he'd disavow the scheme and everybody connected with it. Including me. He'd withdraw from the race." She paused, waiting for Norah to say something.

There was nothing to say.

"It would be the end for us, Lieutenant. I'd lose him."

"You should have thought of that before, Mrs. Barthelmess. Money laundering is a serious crime. Even if I wanted to, there's no way I could help you. Too many people know already. The U.S. Attorney for one. He'll be entering the case."

Mrs. Barthelmess's face twisted with anguish. She licked her lips. "Give me a little time. Give me a chance to tell Will myself. That's not much to ask."

"Who set up the money-laundering scheme?" Norah insisted. "Who approached you? Was it Herrera himself, or someone on his behalf?" Norah was probing, hoping to touch off a reaction. "You didn't just stumble on each other; someone brought you together. Right now that person is trying to protect you, but for how long? He's a man used to making deals. He won't hesitate to sacrifice you if he sees a way to save himself."

Judith Barthelmess remained silent, but obviously she was thinking about what Norah had just said and she would go on thinking about it.

"One more question, Mrs. Barthelmess: where were you on Saturday night between ten-thirty P.M. and midnight?"

"Me? Saturday? Let's see. Yes, I was in my Georgetown office. My secretary and several staff people will vouch for it. We worked late." She tossed it off casually.

"And your husband?"

"Will? Will was in New York most of Friday and Saturday. He got home late Saturday . . . probably around eleven. Yes, I was listening to the eleven o'clock news."

"I suppose by then everybody else had already left."

"Yes, they had."

Norah was certain that Ralph Dreeben was the one who had concocted the money-laundering scheme and brought the principals together, but unless Mrs. Barthelmess was willing to give evidence, she saw no way of implicating him, much less of convicting him.

"The U.S. Attorney wants to talk to you," Manny Jacoby informed Norah as soon as she returned to the station house.

Under the RICO law his entrance into the case was just about inevitable. She'd been expecting his call, even welcomed it.

"I'm still carrying the homicide though." She made it a statement.

"Sure. Just as long as you keep this office advised of your progress."

"Right, Captain." The way it was shaping up, she'd be spending more time keeping the big shots advised than in pursuing the case.

"It's for your own good, Lieutenant."

"I appreciate that, sir."

In the pain for Randall's death and the determination to clear his name and uncover his murderer, Norah was losing sight of the earlier crime, the shooting of Dolores Lopez and the baby. She believed that the clue to both was to be found in the period between Friday afternoon when Randall visited Mrs. Barthelmess in Georgetown and Saturday night when he died in his car on the shoulder of the Grand Central Parkway. Where did he go in the interval? What did he do? Whom did he see? Ralph Dreeben for one. Who else?

On Friday noon, Randall promised Norah a solution to the flea-market murders within forty-eight hours. He had been confident not only of naming the killer, but of providing evidence. Norah recalled the suppressed excitement in his amber eyes. From the very beginning, Randall had insisted the shooting was another incident in the ongoing drug wars. In the course of his investigation he had stumbled onto a bigger story. He had uncovered a political connection. That was after he returned from Puerto Rico. What he learned there was what led him to Judith Barthelmess. She, in turn, willingly or otherwise, directed him to Ralph Dreeben. And after Dreeben? Who else but Will Barthelmess, the man they were all trying to protect?

Randall must have contacted Barthelmess, Norah reasoned and the congressman could ill afford to turn down a journalist of Tye's prominence. No matter how busy he was, he would make time for him. Nor could he turn her down, Norah thought. He would wish to be perceived as cooperative, so he would see her—once. She'd better make the meeting count.

And if she wanted to justify the interrogation to the brass, she'd better get results.

Norah prepared herself, all the while looking over her shoulder at the progress being made by the U.S. Attorney. Al Virgilius was known to be a meticulous investigator. Why shouldn't he be? He had a large staff and they dug deep. He would surely research the congressman's past before making any kind of move on him. Norah counted on Virgilius taking the time for a very thorough preparation. At this point, she was ahead of him, maybe only a couple of steps, but ahead. Once he caught up, he would pass her—easily. And once he had interviewed Barthelmess, she would have lost any leverage she might have had.

Research by computer was easy and fast, if you were experienced and had the necessary access codes. Norah didn't qualify. She did it the old-fashioned way; she went to the Public Library, to the main branch on Forty-second and Fifth.

Millions had been spent on the renovation of the imposing building, and were worth it, Norah decided as she walked along the polished marble corridor to the main reference room. The hushed atmosphere suggested a respect for learning that was heartening. The rows of heads bent to the printed page in the glow of green-shaded reading lamps were cause for hope, Norah thought. She would have enjoyed tracking down the material herself, but she didn't know her way around the files well enough and would be slow. She approached the librarian, Mrs. Violet Winterthal, according to the name plaque on her desk. Mrs. Winterthal, fiftyish and nearsighted, responded by instructing Norah in the use of the files.

Norah interrupted, identified herself as a police officer and again asked for assistance. Sighing lugubriously, the librarian found her a place at one of the tables and placed before her the current *Who's Who in American Politics, Congressional Quarterly's Washington Information Directory*, and a copy of the regular *Who's Who*. From these Norah compiled a biography.

> Barthelmess, William Jason
> U.S. Representative
> b. Elmhurst, Queens, N.Y. Jan. 18, 1947;
> s. Peter H. Barthelmess and Rosemary Grandison B; m.
> 1972 to Judith Ancell. *Service U.S. Armed Forces* 68–70;
> rank, Segt. wounded Vietnam; treated Veterans Hosp.
> B'klyn, NY, dischgd 70. *Educ.* William and Mary,
> Williamsburg, Va. BA, 69, JD, 72; Plit and Govt Ps; Legis.
> asst. to U.S. Congressman T. Elgar, 72–74; to N.Y.
> Assembly 75–76; asst. town supervisor Babylon, N.Y., 78–
> 79; to U.S. House of Representatives Manhattan 19th D.,
> 82. *Honors and Awards* Environ Preservation, 83;
> Conservation Efforts, 85; *Mem* Lions, Treatment
> Alternatives to Street Crime. *Relig.* Presbyterian. *Legal
> Res.* P.O. Box A33 Lenox Hill P.O., N.Y.C.

Out of the jumble of small print and unfamiliar abbreviations, one item jumped out at Norah: Veterans Hospital, Brooklyn. She went back and reviewed the biography, putting service record, education, and marriage into chronological sequence. The way she worked it out, military service had interrupted Barthelmess's education. Wounded, he was returned home and treated at the Veterans Hospital. Released, he went back to school and got his degree. In the course of his studies, he married.

Veterans Hospital in Brooklyn was where Randall had been operated on and then treated.

So had countless others. Norah needed to know if these two had been there at the same time. If it turned out that they had, that was not necessarily proof they'd had any contact, Norah cautioned herself, but her blood coursed hot as she gathered up the material and carried it back to Mrs. Winterthal's desk.

"Thank you," she said. Then, more out of habit than with any real expectation, she asked, "Do you recall anyone else coming in to request the same reference material within the past few days?"

"I'm sorry," the librarian said, shaking her head. How could she be expected to remember such a thing was the question implicit in her attitude. Others might have time for trivia, but she didn't.

"Well, thanks again for your help. If anything should occur to you, you can reach me at this number." She held out one of her cards.

The librarian took it, and the way she looked at it indicated that she was just then acknowledging the official aspect of the request. "As a matter of fact, Lieutenant, someone did ask for a copy of the *Who's Who in American Politics*. I remember because the copy was not immediately available, and this person was not disposed to wait. He worked for one of the TV stations," she stated, as though that explained his impatience. "I didn't speak to him myself; Louise Bertram was helping him. She came to me to ask if we couldn't request a copy from archives! Naturally, it was out of the question."

"Did Miss Bertram mention what station this man worked for?"

The librarian frowned. "I think she said Liberty Network. I think she said the man did research for Randall Tye." Having established that she was not impressed, Mrs. Winterthal was now willing to admit remembering.

"May I speak to Miss Bertram?"

"She's not in today, but I could give you her home address and telephone number."

"I'd appreciate it."

While her fingers tapped through the Rolodex, Mrs. Winterthal, in the habitual hushed tone of the reading room, commented, "What a shocking thing to happen. I mean, not only that he died so suddenly, but the way of it. Mr. Tye seemed like a fine man. I never would have guessed he was an addict. Never. I mean, people like him—they have everything, don't they? And still they look for more. I don't understand. Self-indulgence is what it is. And once you're . . . hooked . . ." she used the word as though it would contaminate her, "I suppose you're never really cured."

Randall was not a drug addict! Norah wanted to tell her. She wanted to shout it at her, shatter the silence of the reading room and with it the woman's smug self-righteousness. But she swallowed the words and the indignation. This was not the time. Soon, though. Soon she would find out what had really happened, and Randall's name would be cleared.

Chapter
SEVENTEEN

The next morning Norah called Representative Barthelmess's Washington office and was told he was in New York and could probably be reached at his campaign headquarters. A little bit of luck, she thought and took the bus across the town to Fifth Avenue and then walked down to the Pierre Hotel. It was a little added luck that Barthelmess was there and his wife wasn't.

He didn't keep her waiting long, five minutes at most, then she was ushered into the typical campaign office—a small, bare room, functionally and minimally furnished, posters of the candidate on the wall, and stacks of campaign literature everywhere else.

"Lieutenant Mulcahaney." He rose from his chair and held out a hand.

He was slim, attractive, forceful, Norah thought; young enough to cause hearts to flutter and old enough to suggest experience and reliability. "Thank you for seeing me, sir. I know how busy you must be."

"There are certain things one has to make time for," the candidate replied with a rueful smile. "I've found that out. I've also found out that sooner makes for less complications later."

Smooth, Norah thought. "I assume you know who Randall Tye was and that he died recently," she began carefully.

"Of course, to both assumptions. The events have been highly publicized."

"Yes." Norah took a breath. "I'm from Homicide, Fourth Division. I'm investigating . . ."

"The death of Randall Tye. Yes. I know who you are, Lieutenant. My wife has told me all about you."

Not all, Norah thought.

"We're puzzled at your interest in us, though. According to everything I've heard and read, Mr. Tye died from an overdose of heroin."

"We're interested in where he got the drug."

"I don't see how we can help you with that."

Norah waited a fraction, then administered the first jolt. "Your wife does a great deal of business with a certain Juan Herrera, a known drug dealer."

His handsome face darkened. "I take that to mean real-estate business. You'll have to discuss it with her. I have no part in it, but I'm sure that whatever she's doing is both legally and morally correct."

"You have complete confidence in her."

"Certainly. To tell you the truth, Lieutenant, I find this a very strange conversation. Unless you can tell me straight out what you're after, the interview is over."

"How well did you know Randall Tye?"

"I didn't know him at all."

"You were a patient at the Veterans Hospital in Brooklyn from February through March 1970. Isn't that correct?"

"Somewhere around then."

"That's what the hospital records show."

"All right. Fine."

"Randall Tye was there at the same time."

"It's a big hospital, Lieutenant, and it was a long time ago."

"Randall Tye's name and face are recognized from coast to coast."

"That may be, but why should I connect a renowned newscaster with some kid in the hospital almost twenty years ago? Maybe if we'd been in the same ward, but we weren't. I was recovering from an infection. According to the stories, he was being treated for morphine addiction."

"Dependency," she corrected. "Brought about because of bungled surgery." Why hadn't he simply said no? Why go into such detail?

"Whatever the reason. I wasn't being judgmental, Lieutenant, only explaining how it was possible for us to have been in the same place at the same time and not have had contact. Do you remember everybody who was . . . in your high school English class, for instance?"

"But when he came to see you, didn't you recognize him then?"

Barthelmess didn't answer right away. He had options: he could deny any meeting had taken place, or he could take a forthright attitude, acknowledge and explain. He chose the latter.

"I recognized him as the news anchor for the Liberty Network."

"You must have been on the debating team in school," Norah commented wryly.

"It's the congressional training, Lieutenant." Barthelmess smiled deprecatingly. Then the smile faded. "You're wasting time, yours and mine. Please get to the point."

"The point is that we are dealing with two crimes: illegal money laundering and homicide. Yes, sir, the indications are that Randall Tye's death was neither accident nor suicide. I am not directly concerned with the money laundering; the U.S. Attorney will be dealing with that. The evidence against Mrs. Barthelmess is very strong on that, and it was Randall Tye who uncovered that evidence. So she had a motive for getting rid of him—and that's where I come in."

Will Barthelmess's boyish face sagged, yellowed, the jowls hung like dewlaps and he looked as though he had jumped the intervening years into old age. He knew he was being offered a chance to shift suspicion from his wife. He hesitated.

"Of course, there are others involved," Norah went on. "Ralph Dreeben for one. He's at the end of a respected career; if his connection to the money-laundering scheme were revealed, he stood to lose his reputation. Juan Herrera would be looking at a long jail term. It's a question of values, Mr. Barthelmess. Your wife stood to lose more than either of them. She stood to lose you."

Barthelmess bowed his head. He covered his face with both hands and stayed that way.

Norah decided she'd waited long enough.

"And you stood to lose everything."

"Me?" He looked up. It was the most severe of the jolts, but he didn't flinch.

"You stood to lose your reputation and your career. You benefited like the others, maybe more. Who will believe you didn't know what was going on? And if you knew, then you condoned. Randall Tye threatened to break the story. It would have destroyed you."

Barthelmess swallowed. He took a handkerchief from his back pocket and wiped his face. Then he fished a cigarette from a pack lying at the corner of the desk and lit up.

"You're a smart woman, Lieutenant Mulcahaney, and intuitive, too. I realize that my wife is in big trouble and what you say is true—nobody is going to believe that I'm not in it with her right up to my eyebrows.

So we're going to have to pay, both of us. But laundering drug money and committing murder are two different things; neither Judith nor I had anything to do with Randall Tye's death."

He took a couple of drags on the cigarette.

"I remembered Tye from the hospital. A celebrity like him, of course I did. He didn't remember me. I'm just one of five hundred and thirty-five or so members of the House. He didn't remember until I reminded him. It was a complication he wasn't prepared for."

Norah frowned. She didn't understand.

"Tye contacted me . . . let's see, Saturday afternoon right here. He wanted an interview. He didn't indicate what line he intended to take, but I had a feeling somehow it wouldn't be an ordinary interview and I decided I didn't want him coming here. I certainly didn't want what I sensed would be a confrontation to take place in my Washington office. I decided it should be somewhere we could both retain our anonymity. I'd planned to go home that evening, so I suggested we meet at the airport. He agreed. We met at the ticket counter, and from there we went into the bar. You know how crowded those places are, but just the same a couple of people spotted Tye. Nobody wasted a second glance at me."

That explained Randall's using his own car and driving himself, Norah thought.

"We found a booth and Tye didn't waste any time confronting me with what he had. He said he was giving me a chance to defend myself by telling him the whole story. He offered to depict Judith as an innocent dupe and to exonerate me of any knowledge of the scheme. I made him a counteroffer: his silence regarding my wife's involvement in the money laundering and the source of my campaign funds, in return for my silence about his drug addiction. I figured each of us had a comparable amount to lose. He accepted."

Norah was stunned.

"We shook hands on it and went our ways—I caught the next flight back home to Washington and I assumed he went back to Manhattan."

Still numb from the shock, Norah was beginning slowly to gather her wits. "How long would you say the meeting lasted?"

Barthelmess shrugged. The question seemed pointless, but he answered. "Not long. Maybe fifteen, twenty minutes."

She didn't know herself where she was headed. "That's all?"

"I think so."

"Hardly even time to order anything. I assume you did order?"

"Certainly."

"What? What did you order? Who picked up the tab?"

"Really . . . I don't remember."

"Please try."

He frowned. "I probably had a Perrier. I usually do. And he had a beer. As I recall, he paid. Left a couple of bills on the table when we were through."

"You did say the bar was crowded."

"Yes, yes. What are you after, Lieutenant?"

"Only that it seems to me you must have been there longer than fifteen or twenty minutes. I mean, if the bar was crowded it would take a while for your order to be brought to you. You'd hardly have time to consume your drinks, much less transact your business."

"No, the waitress was prompt. We had plenty of time for both."

"You finished your Perrier and Randall drank his beer?"

"Yes, Lieutenant, I've told you."

"And you left the bar together?"

"Yes, again. I went directly to the departure gate and he headed for the parking lot."

Norah pounced. "How did you know that was where he was going?"

Barthelmess blinked. "I assumed . . . It was in the papers that he was found in his car."

"Much later. And by the side of the road, not in the parking lot. And headed *toward* the airport."

"He mentioned he was going to drive out. In fact, he'd offered me a ride when we arranged the meeting, but my schedule was too uncertain and I didn't accept."

"I see," Norah nodded. "Again, which flight was it that you took?"

He sighed. "Nine o'clock."

"Ah. I don't think you mentioned that. However, is there any way you can prove you were on that flight—since there's no passenger list or seat reservation? Was there someone on the plane you knew?"

Barthelmess frowned. "The stewardess." His brow cleared. "She recognized me. Apparently, I'd flown with her before."

"Is that so? How fortunate. What's her name?"

He thought about it. "Ah . . . it was a somewhat unusual name . . . Celestine. That's it."

"How about when you landed? Did somebody meet you?"

"No. My car was at the airport. I drove myself straight home, but there was a lot of traffic, so I didn't get there till some time around eleven. My wife was waiting up for me."

"Anybody else there? Friends, campaign staff? Your au pair girl?"

"No, they were all gone by then."

"So we'll just have to find Celestine," Norah said.

No way Randall would have made a deal with Barthelmess, Norah thought. She plain did not believe it.

To start with, Randall had been right up front about his stay in the Veterans Hospital and the reason for it. He hadn't advertised it, but it was right there on his bio for anybody who took the trouble to discover. If Barthelmess had followed up his threat to make the newscaster's past dependency public, sympathy would have come down heavily on Randall's side, Norah thought. He could have ridden out the scandal, but Barthelmess could not have shaken free of the criminal connection.

At least, that was Norah's opinion. She was also well aware that a preoccupation with drugs gripped society. It had reached the point where just the accusation of drug use, no documentation or evidence required, was enough to destroy a career. At that very moment, a bitter political campaign was in progress in Texas, the result of which could well turn on one candidate's answer to the question: Have you ever used illegal drugs?

The public attitude seemed more forgiving toward sports figures and show-business stars, but there, too, the tide was turning. One misstep might be forgiven, but after that there was little mercy. Randall would fall into that category. And what if there was more to the story? What if Randall had done something under the influence that would be even more devastating if it came to be known?

Norah had hoped that the threat of a homicide charge might frighten the congressman into telling the truth as the lesser of two evils. And it had nearly worked. She'd sensed that he was on the verge, then at the last moment he'd pulled back. At least she now knew where and with whom Randall had been prior to his death. She'd borne down hard on the consumption of drinks at the bar because that was the logical place and time for the Seconal to have been administered.

Working always on the premise that Randall had not voluntarily taken the heroin and that he had not made any deal with Barthelmess, what had happened after the two men left the bar? Norah wondered.

They separated. Randall went to his car, paid his parking fee, and pulled out to the highway and headed for Manhattan. En route, he began to feel drowsy, so he pulled over and passed out.

Only one thing wrong with that, Norah thought, the car, when discovered, was headed the wrong way—not to Manhattan but back to the airport.

Her next job was to check Barthelmess's alibi. There was a small airline terminal right around the corner from the hotel on Fifth. She sought out the manager, who referred her to the operations office at LaGuardia. In this day of technical sophistication, calling up the information she wanted on the computer should have been routine. But, of course, the computer was down. So she'd go home, pick up her car, and drive out.

Her beeper signaled.

"Shoot-out at the corner of Ninety-sixth and Columbus," Arenas informed her. "So far the count is three of the gunmen dead and five bystanders wounded, including an eighty-year-old woman and a ten-year-old boy."

According to witnesses, Ferdi said, the shooting started with an argument over drugs.

Again, she thought. And yet again.

The dispute between Marcello Betancourt, twenty-two, Raul Serrano, thirty-four, and Alberto Rodriguez, twenty-six, began shortly after eleven A.M., a few doors from where Serrano lived. Betancourt pulled a gun, shot Serrano in the leg and fled. Rodriguez, Serrano's buddy, produced a 9mm Uzi and gave chase. About a block from the original shooting, Betancourt ducked into an empty building. Rodriguez followed; fire was exchanged.

When it was over, Betancourt and his cohorts were dead. Three of the bystanders were treated on the spot, but the elderly woman, owner of the corner newsstand where the original argument had broken out, sustained a serious wound in the shoulder, and the ten-year-old boy, who had been buying a comic book from her, was shot in the stomach.

Norah stayed until the injured were transported to St. Luke's–Roosevelt Hospital for treatment, and the bodies of Betancourt and the others were placed in the morgue van for transport.

It was close to three and she hadn't eaten. She also hadn't thought about Randall.

After a quick bite of tunafish on toast at a nearby luncheonette, she returned to the squad. The shoot-out presented no mystery. The crime had been witnessed and the perps identified. For once bystanders had not been afraid to come forward. That was heartening, Norah thought. Maybe the tide of fear and hopelessness was receding. Norah reviewed the paperwork as it came in, wrote up her own report, and headed for home.

After changing into an old pair of slacks and T-shirt, she picked up where she had left off in her reconstruction of the events of the last night of Randall's life. If Randall had made the deal with Barthelmess, there would have been no need for Barthelmess to slip him a mickey. So that part of the congressman's story was a lie. How about the rest of it? How about his alibi? It could hold and he could still be guilty, if he'd had an accomplice, someone waiting at the side for the result of the meeting. If Randall turned down the deal, Barthelmess would give the signal, get on the plane and fly away, leaving the accomplice to take over.

It was not likely the accomplice could get to Randall's car in the lot before he did; certainly not likely he could break in and hide there. He could have had his own car and waited to follow Randall. There were, then, two possibilities: The Seconal which Randall had ingested would cause him to lose control and crash, saving trouble all around, or he'd start to feel drowsy and pull over, which, apparently, was what had happened. The accomplice would then pull in behind him, enter the car, and administer the fatal injection.

Who was the accomplice?

In order to answer that, Norah would have to know when Barthelmess found out what was going on. He had told her he had no idea where his campaign funds were coming from till Randall Tye confronted him. But if that were so, then why was he prepared with the counteroffer, or counterthreat? Barthelmess had to know before the meeting. When and how did he find out?

From Dreeben? Dreeben was the one Judith had turned to after her interview with Norah. But by the time Dreeben complained to Chief Deland, Randall was already dead. If he had killed Randall, was it likely he would call attention to himself?

Maybe Dreeben decided it was time to shake Will Barthelmess out of his fantasies and let him face the reality of politics. Dreeben was, after all, Barthelmess's chief supporter. Wily and self-serving, clinging to the shreds of his power, he might have decided it was time for the candidate to help his own cause. Dreeben could very well have been the one to concoct the entire scheme.

"See Tye and offer him the deal," Dreeben might have counseled. "If he won't go for it, slip a couple of these into his drink. Harmless, they'll knock him out is all. Then give me the high sign, and I'll take it from there."

But Dreeben wasn't the one who followed Randall and administered the injection. He had an alibi. Of sorts.

He could have called in Juan Herrera. Why not? Who more logical? The drug dealer was at the apex of the triangle of conspiracy. Setting up a scheme to put tainted money into circulation required ingenuity and connections, "straight" connections. Compared to that, dealing was routine. It would be natural for Herrera to use drugs as a weapon. Norah didn't believe that Barthelmess would work directly with the drug dealer, but he didn't have to know who was actually going to take Randall out. There was no reason for Dreeben to tell him.

Always, always the primary concern appeared to be to protect the congressman. Norah caught herself starting to doze off, blinked, and pulled herself up. She needed to check Will Barthelmess's alibi. Although Norah was convinced he would not have mentioned the stewardess if he weren't absolutely certain she would support his story, Norah had to talk to her. Tomorrow she thought, first thing.

Elbows on the desk, Norah rested her head in her hands: Consider the relationship between Barthelmess and his wife; consider how determined Judith had been to keep the real purpose of her job at Executive Transfers secret. What would her reaction have been when she learned that he had been told? She would have been distraught and anxious to justify herself to him. Would she have rushed back to New York to talk to Randall once more? To plead with him to keep the secret?

Suppose it was Judith who approached Randall when he left the airport bar? He wouldn't have been afraid of her. She might even have asked for a ride back to the city and he would have said yes. Once in the car, she might have kept him talking till the mickey took effect, then pushed him over and taken the wheel herself and driven to a place where she could administer the injection.

No, no, no. Something was wrong with that. It couldn't have happened that way. She was getting muddled, Norah thought. She closed her eyes.

For the second time that week Norah was awakened by the ringing of the telephone in the night. She raised her head. According to her watch it was three-twelve A.M. The phone rang again. She picked it up.

"Lieutenant? It's Ferdi."

Ferdi was working the four-to-midnight and should have been home and in bed which, from the sounds in the background, he obviously was not. "What've you got?"

"Congressman Barthelmess just reported the death of his wife. It looks like suicide."

Norah felt as though the breath had been knocked out of her. Slowly, deeply, she sucked in air.

"Where?"

"The Plaza Hotel."

"I'm on my way."

Chapter

EIGHTEEN

The lobby of the elegant hotel was softly lit, quiet, empty. There was no indication that somewhere on an upper floor, in one of the luxurious suites, a woman lay dead. Norah supposed that management policy was to insulate the guests from disturbances of every kind, even death. She identified herself to the desk clerk and was directed to the elevators around the corner, past the Oak Room, and up to the sixth floor.

The sixth floor, however, was far from normal, though it was quiet enough under the circumstances. Uniformed police were posted at the elevators and the stairwell exits. Two civilians, probably the night manager and the head of security, paced in front of the door to the crime scene. They frowned when Norah got off the elevator, was acknowledged by the officer, and approached. They wanted the police to be gone, not to have more come. They had no choice but to stand aside.

Norah passed through a small vestibule and into a large, well-proportioned living room. Will Barthelmess sat in a far corner, his head in his hands. He didn't look up. Norah, responding to a signal from Ferdi Arenas, passed by without speaking and entered the bedroom.

The coverlet had been removed, folded neatly, and set to one side. The covers had been turned down; by the maid, probably, Norah thought. Judith Barthelmess, fully dressed except for her shoes, lay on top. Preparing to die, if she had been preparing to die, she had taken care not to get dirt on the bedclothes. She looked peaceful, Norah thought.

By this time, the full complement of crime-scene personnel had assembled and was going about the business of examining and recording. The photographers first, flashbulbs popping. After them, assistant ME

Carl Lese (Chief Worgan would not roll on this one, not when there was a strong assumption of suicide). While Lese made his examination, forensics dusted for prints on likely surfaces. In due course they would tag and remove items for evidence. At the moment, those were the empty glass on the bedside table, the plastic prescription vial beside it, and the open, handwritten letter. Through it all, Judith Barthelmess appeared to be quietly sleeping.

Norah squinted, fished in her purse in the compartment next to her gun, and found her reading glasses. Then she picked up the note by the upper right-hand corner and read:

> To the police and the U.S. Attorney,
> My husband, Will Barthelmess, had no knowledge of my activities. He had no idea that the money I supplied to his campaign for the Senate was illegally obtained. He is completely innocent of any involvement.
> Randall Tye uncovered the scheme. I killed him to keep the secret. I met Tye at the airport and put knockout drops in his drink. Then I asked him to give me a ride to the city. By the time we got to the car he was ready to pass out. I injected him with heroin.
> I'm sorry to have destroyed his reputation, but he would have destroyed Will's.

Norah went back and read the letter again. "Did you see this?" she asked the assistant ME.

"Yes."

"Do you buy it?"

He was surprised by the question. A recent addition to the medical examiner's staff, Carl Lese was one of the new, young, bright pathologists Phil Worgan had hired in his reorganization of the office. "As far as I can tell at this stage, it's medically consistent." Lese was not committed to the belief in medical infallibility, so he added, "Why? Do you know something I don't?"

She did, but for the moment decided to keep it to herself. "Something about the letter. It doesn't feel right."

"A person contemplating suicide isn't normal," Lese pointed out. "She might already have taken the drug before she started composing. You'll get the handwriting checked, of course."

"Of course." Norah turned to Ferdi. "This is all? She didn't leave a letter for her husband?"

"I didn't see any."

"Who found her?"

"He did."

Norah walked back to the living room followed by Arenas.

"Mr. Barthelmess, I'm very sorry for your loss."

He looked up, seemingly very little affected by her presence. "Thank you, Lieutenant."

"I wish I didn't have to trouble you at this time."

"I know. I understand. Go ahead."

"Was Mrs. Barthelmess unusually depressed recently?"

"You know the answer to that, Lieutenant: she most certainly was. I'm not blaming you; you were only doing your job, but your allegations were deeply disturbing to her. That should be obvious from the letter, if you didn't know already."

Norah decided not to respond directly. "What time did you and Mrs. Barthelmess check in to the hotel today?"

"We didn't need to check in. We've been maintaining this suite for the period of the campaign."

"But your headquarters are at the Pierre."

"The office space we required was not available here."

"I see. Would you mind giving me an account of your activities today, Mr. Barthelmess?"

"Not at all. In the morning, I was at the NBC studios in Rockefeller Center to tape three new campaign spots. In late afternoon, I toured the Bronx. I came back here to shower and change for a dinner at the Odyssey Club on Sixty-eighth."

"Your wife accompanied you to each of these events?"

"No, she spent most of the day at our Forty-second Street office organizing our telephone-registration drive. She called to say she was running late and not feeling all that well and had decided to skip the dinner. It wasn't particularly important for her to be there."

"So you didn't see her before you left?"

"Oh, I saw her. She came in while I was dressing and I asked her once again if she wouldn't change her mind and come with me. She said no. She intended to order dinner from room service and then go right to bed."

"I see. And what time did you return from the affair?"

"The dinner was over by ten-thirty," he told her with a look that indicated he was well ahead of her. "I was charged up and I didn't feel like going back to the room so early. It was a nice night and I decided to take a walk. I wandered over to Third Avenue. I found a little bar that looked friendly and stopped in for a couple of drinks." He looked her straight in the eyes. "I don't know the name of the bar, but I could probably find it again, if I had to."

Of course, Norah thought. She had no doubt that he would produce the location as conveniently as he had remembered the name of the stewardess on his nine o'clock flight, when it suited him. It would suit him after he had a chance to talk to the bartender.

"Do you recall what time you got back to the Plaza?"

"A little before one."

No hesitation there, probably because he knew he had been observed coming in, Norah decided.

"You didn't place the call to 911 till just before three A.M."

"That's right. Yes. When I came in, the door to the bedroom was closed and no light showed. I opened it a crack and looked in. I could make out that Judith was on the bed and, I assumed, asleep. I didn't want to wake her, so I closed the door. I fixed myself another drink, turned on the television, low, and sat for a while." He indicated a highball glass on the cocktail table. It was half full, the melted ice diluting the amber color to a pale yellow. "I must have dozed off. I woke abruptly, as one does, in a cramped and uncomfortable position. By my watch it was twenty to three. I turned off the television and tiptoed into the bedroom.

"I didn't turn on the light for fear of disturbing Judith. I just left the connecting door open so I could see to get undressed. While I was doing that I noticed that Judith was unnaturally still. In fact, she was in exactly the same position she'd been in when I first came home, lying on her side with her back toward me."

And now she was lying flat on her back, Norah reflected.

"I think for one split second my heart stopped. Then I turned on the light and went around to where I could look directly into her face. Her eyes were closed. She didn't appear to be breathing. I felt for a pulse and couldn't find any. I turned her over and tried to give her mouth-to-mouth resuscitation. She didn't respond. Her skin felt cold and clammy."

He paused and sighed deeply. "Then I saw the empty prescription vial and water glass. And, of course, the letter. After that I called 911."

"Was that the only letter? Was there a separate message for you?"

"No."

Norah paused and studied him before deciding to go on. "Your wife didn't do it; she didn't kill Randall Tye. When he died Mrs. Barthelmess was in her Georgetown office surrounded by an assortment of campaign workers. She had an alibi. She's the only one who had an alibi that would stand up."

"Then why did she confess?"

Norah looked hard at him. "Because she loved you."

He seemed surprised. His face twisted with uncertainty. "When I first looked in, if I'd turned the light on then, could she have been saved, do you think?"

"I can't answer that," Norah said. She didn't tell him the answer might come with the autopsy; he knew that. She wasn't sure it was really important to him.

The confession stood.

Narcotics was busy making a case against Juan Herrera.

The U.S. Attorney's office was conducting an in-depth investigation of Executive Transfers and Ralph Dreeben's and Judith Barthelmess's illegal activities. So far, Representative Barthelmess appeared to have clean hands.

Public sympathy weighed in on his side—due largely to his wife's sacrifice. If Judith Barthelmess was willing to die to preserve her husband's good name, he must be innocent. That was the general consensus. At the initial revelation, there had been shock and outrage. Barthelmess had immediately announced his intention of withdrawing from the senatorial race, even resigning his seat in the House. But he kept putting it off. As the days passed, it became apparent that he would not resign.

The furor died down and though Barthelmess was certainly not campaigning actively, he didn't say any more about backing out. After a while, it was taken for granted that he would put his name before the voters and let the people judge him.

They might even elect him, Norah thought. She marveled at the public's tolerance. Hadn't there been a Boston mayor who had been reelected while serving a jail term?

Meanwhile, Randall Tye was vindicated. His colleagues eulogized him on the air and in print. His only living relative, his sister, a frumpy housewife from Sioux City, Iowa, turned up. She was uncomfortable in the company of her famous brother's famous friends. She wanted only to claim his body and slip away as quickly as possible for a quiet, private funeral at home. The network wouldn't hear of it, not till after a lavish memorial service. Five hundred personalities from every field of entertainment and communications attended. One after the other the celebrities went to the podium to eulogize Tye. Outside the church, police had to be called to control the crowds. When it was over, only the sister, Jeff Higgins, head of his research staff, and Norah remained for a private farewell.

Norah walked over to the sister. "Mrs. Spach? I'm Norah Mulcahaney. I was a friend of Randall's."

For a moment, a smile lit the pudgy, tear-swollen face. "He told me about you. Every time he called, he talked about you. He said he would bring you out one day so we could meet."

"Did he?" Norah was deeply touched.

Elsie Spach nodded and the tears welled up again. "It was a beautiful ceremony, wasn't it?"

"Oh, yes."

"I won't be able to do anything near so fancy for him back in Sioux City. But it will be nice for him to be near Ma and Pa, don't you think? They'll keep each other company. And I'll visit with them." She paused. "Maybe you could come out once in a while?"

Norah nodded. "I'll come."

Doubts continued to nag Norah. How convenient that Judith Barthelmess had killed herself, she thought. It was the suicide note that troubled her. Not only had Mrs. Barthelmess supplied few details of the crime, but the tone was cold, almost impersonal. She never spoke of her love for her husband. She never addressed him directly, not even to say goodbye.

She discussed it with Captain Jacoby.

Manny Jacoby scowled. "She gave her life for him. What more could she do? Are you suggesting the letter's not genuine?"

"Oh, it's genuine all right."

"Well then?" He relaxed, but not for long. "Obviously, you think she lied, but why would she?" He almost wished he hadn't asked, but the

Norah Mulcahaney he knew was going to tell him, whether he wanted to hear it or not.

"She would only lie to protect him." Norah's blue eyes bored into his.

"What about Barthelmess's alibi? He claims the stewardess on the plane will remember him."

"Very clearly."

"So he made a point of calling attention to himself." Jacoby shrugged. "Have you talked to her?"

"Not yet."

"What are you waiting for?"

"She's taking a long weekend in the Caribbean."

"So, when she gets back talk to her, clear it up."

"Yes, sir. Another thing bothers me, Captain: the time lapse on the night of the alleged suicide. Barthelmess's dinner at the Odyssey Club was over by ten-thirty. He claims he went for a walk and ended up in some bar on Third. He got back to his hotel just before one. The night clerk remembers him coming in at that time. The question is—where was he in the interim?"

Grunting, Jacoby leaned back in his chair, stretched out his legs, and settled himself. He might as well hear it all.

"Mrs. Barthelmess's movements on that night are also interesting," Norah continued. "According to her husband, she came in while he was dressing for the dinner. He asked her once again if she wouldn't change her mind and accompany him, but she said no, she intended to order dinner up from room service and then go right to bed. When we answered the complaint, there was no food trolley. I interviewed the room-service captain and he confirmed a meal had been ordered and delivered to the suite at eight P.M. At approximately nine-thirty, the waiter went up to remove the trolley, but there was no answer to his knock. He waited, knocked again, then used his passkey.

"The sitting room was empty. The bedroom door was open and he could see there was no one there, either. The meal had been eaten, so he wheeled away what was left and locked the door behind him."

"She could have been in the bathroom."

"That was dark, too."

"So she went out for a breath of air."

"She went out all right, but not for air. The doorman got her a taxi.

He remembers her not because she's the candidate's wife, but because she tipped well and took the trouble to remember his name."

"Where did she go?"

"The doorman didn't hear the address she gave the driver."

Manny Jacoby considered. Chief Deland had given precise orders to stay clear of Judith and Will Barthelmess and Ralph Dreeben, to leave them strictly alone. Mrs. Barthelmess's death changed the situation. Suicide or murder, he was fully justified in ordering Mulcahaney to go ahead with the investigation.

"So locate the driver. Put some people on it. You can't do everything yourself."

Chapter NINETEEN

Manny Jacoby having officially untied her hands, Norah went ahead and put Ferdi Arenas on the job of tracing the cabbie. It wasn't difficult. There was a hack stand just around the corner from the main entrance of the Plaza, and the regulars were well known to the doormen. In no time at all Ferdi had the man he wanted—Sayed Kahn, an Indian medical student who was moonlighting. When Ferdi started questioning him he seemed nervous and at the same time relieved.

"I have been wondering whether I should come forward, Officer," Sayed Kahn admitted, his large, liquid eyes fixed on the sergeant. "I read about what happened to the lady passenger, but . . ."

"Why didn't you come forward?"

He was sweating. "She gave me a very large tip. I was afraid if my dispatcher found out I would have to share it."

"Found out what?"

"I justified my silence by saying to myself that I had not taken her to the place of her death, but rather away from it. But in my heart I knew I was reasoning speciously."

"Mr. Kahn, please, just tell me what happened."

"Well, the lady you're asking about, whose picture you showed me? I took her to the Odyssey Club on Sixty-eighth Street. When we got there she had me pull up across from the entrance and told me to wait. She said it might be a while and she gave me twenty dollars. She promised me twenty more when she came out. I said I was not permitted to do that unless I kept the meter running, so she said all right, keep it running." He looked to Ferdi for support. "I didn't see anything wrong with that."

Ferdi nodded.

"She went inside. I sat there for nearly half an hour, taking the opportunity to do some studying, when suddenly she was back, pulling the door open and pointing to a cab moving past us toward Madison. She told me to follow, but not to let them know we were following. I did my best."

"Go on."

"When the cab we were following reached its destination and let its passenger out, she ordered me to drive on for another half block. Then she paid me and waved me off."

"The passenger of the other cab, was it a man?"

"Yes."

"Did you recognize him? Can you describe him?"

"It was dark and I just drove by. He was tall, thin, wearing a tuxedo."

"How about the address? Do you have the address where he got off?"

"No, sir. But I can show you. I can show you the building."

It was a small, recently renovated apartment house between York and First. It had been gutted and the shell reconstructed with new wiring, plumbing, and insulation. There was no doorman, not even a superintendent on the premises; nonetheless, it was considered a luxury building. Certainly the tenants paid luxury prices and the forty apartments were fully occupied. Security was provided by a closed-circuit television system. The team, consisting of Arenas, Wyler, Neel, and Ochs, set about interviewing each and every tenant. The pretext was that they were insurance investigators working for a prospective buyer who wanted an independent assessment of the condition of the building. After two days, the detectives had canvassed thirty-nine of them. The fortieth, Mrs. Charles Hunt, was not at home, though they'd tried several times at different hours of the day and night.

So the thirty-nine bells were rung again and the tenants questioned about Mrs. Hunt.

She did not occupy the apartment on a regular basis, the detectives learned. She was rich, single, and did a lot of traveling: that was the opinion of the other three tenants on that same floor. A young couple who had run into Mrs. Hunt occasionally in the hall on the way to the incinerator chute, described her as reclusive. They speculated she was recently widowed. She did have a male visitor—infrequently. He came at night and they had no idea whether he stayed over or not. No one had been close enough to even attempt a description. As for Mrs. Hunt, they had run into her in the hall and elevator; they had exchanged pleasantries. So once again Norah resorted to the use of a police artist. Revealing the police interest in the elusive Mrs. Hunt, she now asked the neighbors to work with the artist. When they were through, everyone agreed that the result—a dark-haired, sultry woman in her mid-twenties—was an excellent likeness. To Norah and the team she was instantly recognizable.

Carmen Herrera.

So it was back full circle to the flea-market shooting.

Everyone, including herself, seemed to have forgotten about the ruthless gunning down of Dolores Lopez and the baby, Carmen's baby, Norah thought and felt a tightening around her heart. For all that she'd denied being the baby's mother, Carmen had made no secret of her love for Charlito. She remembered Carmen, tears streaming down her face, as she ran across the schoolyard. She remembered Carmen reaching into the carriage and clutching the bloody infant to her bosom. Oh, she'd cared. After the initial eruption of despair, Carmen Herrera had regained her control and maintained it ever since. She had withdrawn, but Norah believed it was only to await the opportune moment. Carmen had no intention of letting the murder of her sister and of her baby go unavenged.

That's it! Norah thought with a surge of elation.

She had it at last, the direction she'd been searching for and which had been right there in plain sight from the very beginning: the crux of the case—Carmen's love for her infant son. She was the kind who would act indirectly, using others to do her will.

Didn't Randall get his first intimation that the Barthelmess campaign was linked to drugs when he went to see Carmen in Mayagüez? It was Carmen who had put him on to it, Norah thought, knowing exactly where it would lead.

On the basis of the Identikit portrait of the woman calling herself Mrs. Charles Hunt, Norah was able to get a search warrant and enter the Hunt apartment. She wanted to be as unobtrusive as possible, so she went in taking only Ferdi with her, and choosing mid-morning as the hour when most of the tenants were likely to be out.

All pale-beige and white, Apartment 9A looked as though it had been directly transported from Bloomingdale's furniture department, down to the last toss pillow and ashtray. Considering the lengths to which the Hunts had gone to keep their identities secret, they had been remarkably lax once they entered the apartment and shut the door behind them. The bedroom closets contained a wide selection of clothing, men's and women's. There was a complete supply of toilet articles. Books, magazines, patent medicines, the odds and ends one accumulates as a matter of course testified to the length and intimacy of the relationship. But it was on the verge of dissolution. That was clearly indicated by the gap in the orderly row of men's apparel in the closet, absence of shaving kit, toothbrush, and colognes from the bathroom, empty drawers in the man's chest. Charles Hunt had started to move out.

Not so Mrs. Hunt. Her closet remained full. An untidy assortment of cosmetics cluttered the dressing table. Her bureau drawers were filled with undergarments of satin and lace. On the night table a color snapshot in an elaborate silver frame caught Norah's attention right away. "Ferdi," she called.

"Carmen and the baby," he said instantly. Then hesitated, "And the baby's father?"

"That would be my guess," Norah agreed.

"You think Judith Barthelmess saw this?"

Norah nodded. "She saw it and it broke her heart." She took a deep breath. "Judith must have suspected what was going on, probably had for a long time. Finally, she decided she had to know for sure. She ducked the fund-raiser that last night on purpose, hoping that Will would take the opportunity to meet his lover. As it happened, Carmen was still in Mayagüez, but Will decided it was a good time to come over here and start cleaning out his stuff."

"And while he was at it, his wife appeared on the doorstep."

"Right."

"How did she know which apartment he was in?"

Norah stared at him nonplussed. She couldn't answer, and for a couple of minutes she was silent. She was certain that Judith had been here and that she had left traces of her presence, most likely fingerprints. That would be enough to make the case, but for her own satisfaction Norah couldn't ignore Ferdi's question.

"Well . . . in following her husband, Judith had to stay far enough behind so that he wouldn't spot her, but close enough so as not to lose him. She didn't enter the building till she was sure he was in the elevator. The indicator stopped at nine. She came up after him. When she got off, she was confronted by four apartments, four closed, blank doors." Norah paused. "What could she do but start ringing bells? If a stranger answered, she could just say it was a mistake—she'd got off at the wrong floor, got the wrong apartment number—apologize and try again."

Ferdi shook his head. "I don't think Barthelmess would come to the door. Why wouldn't he just wait till she went away?"

"Because he heard the door buzzers and recognized her voice and knew she wouldn't go away. She was too charged up. She would cause a commotion and he couldn't afford that. He had to admit her.

"There was a bitter confrontation. Each accused the other and tried to justify his own actions. I'm sure Barthelmess pointed to his cleaning out his belongings as proof that the affair was over.

"Judith wanted to believe it, and perhaps she would have if not for this photograph. No argument or justification from Will could avail against the child's resemblance to him." Handling it carefully so as not to mar the highly polished silver frame or spoil the discernible prints, Norah placed it in an evidence envelope and sealed it. Those prints were surely Judith Barthelmess's, and they would be proof not only that she had been here, but that she knew about the affair.

"There was nothing left for her. She went back to the hotel and swallowed every sleeping pill in the medicine cabinet."

"And Barthelmess just let her go?" Ferdi asked.

"To be fair, I don't think he realized how deeply hurt she was. I think he figured that if he left her alone for a while, she'd quiet down. She was a reasonable woman and their lives were linked on several levels. Destroying one meant destroying both. He was sure she'd see all that and her good sense would take over. So he let her go and waited. But he waited too long. By the time he got back to the suite and decided to turn on the light and talk to her . . . it was too late."

"She killed herself and with her dying words absolved him?"

"Yes."

"Women!" Ferdi shook his head.

"The more worthless the man, the greater the obsession."

* * *

The search continued, routinely.

"Lieutenant! Norah!" Ferdi cried out. He stood on a stepstool, examining the top shelf of Barthelmess's closet. He came down carrying a suitcase which he now opened to show her.

Norah stared. "Well, well," she said. "And that's certainly no toy."

Learning from the airline that Celestine Fitzroy was back from vacation, Norah drove out to the beachside rental house she shared with another stewardess. It was a Box and Cox situation, with the schedules balanced so that Celestine was flying when her roommate was on the ground and vice versa. They must both like the beach, Norah thought as she came off the Atlantic Beach bridge and turned right toward the ocean; the house was just across from the beach entrance. Norah parked and went up the walk to the front door and rang. No answer. She'd been told Celestine Fitzroy wasn't flying today and was most probably at home. She rang again, then stepped around to an uncurtained window and peered inside.

In contrast to the hard, white glare of the sun, the interior was dark, and at first Norah could hardly distinguish shapes. After a while, she identified a studio apartment setup. The furniture was spare, Scandinavian style, tile floor, convertible sofa open with the bedclothes tumbled. A wall of appliances on the far side constituted the kitchen. Jeans, underwear, panty hose, and a couple of bathing suits were strewn at random.

"Can I help you?"

Norah jumped and turned to face a slim, blonde, tanned, not young but very attractive woman in white shorts and a red-and-white checked shirt.

"I'm looking for Celestine Fitzroy."

The woman, who was already regarding her with disapproval, now seemed even more displeased. "She's probably on the beach."

"Thank you." Norah came away from the window and started toward the beach entrance.

"You can't get on the beach without a pass."

"That won't be a problem," Norah said.

"And you can't leave your car on the street." The woman pointed to the sign. "There's no parking."

Norah held up her open shield case. "I'll gladly move my car if you'll tell me where it is legal."

But now the woman was all smiles. "I'm so sorry, Officer. I didn't know. I thought . . ." She spread out her hands in a gesture of helplessness. "People come to this house at all hours. They drive up; they walk up; they blow their horns, play their car radios—loud! I thought you . . . well, I guess you know what I thought you were looking for."

"Have you reported the situation?"

"They say they can't do anything till we have evidence. How can we get evidence? If the police can't, how can you expect us to?"

She was angry and frustrated and more—frightened.

"I'll see what I can do," Norah said. It wasn't the answer she would have liked to give.

Finally, Norah was on the beach, walking across the dazzling white sand to the water. On that wide expanse there were perhaps a half-dozen colored umbrellas and no more than a dozen sunbathers; it was still too cold to go into the water. She had been given a description, and now looking over the various groups, she was able to locate the stewardess. She was alone.

"Ms. Fitzroy?"

She was attractive but thin, too thin, Norah thought, almost gaunt. Her cheek bones were pronounced, her jawline sharp, her black hair severely pulled back. She wore a black bathing suit, one-piece, cut high on the hips. Her skin, already deeply tanned, glistened with oil, and she lay on a beach towel soaking up more harmful rays. Her eyes were closed.

"Celestine Fitzroy?"

She opened her eyes and regarded Norah warily. "Yes?"

It was hard to say how old she was; the sun accelerated aging, Norah thought and decided to peg her at the late twenties. "Lieutenant Mulcahaney, Fourth Division."

"Fourth Division what?"

"Homicide," Norah replied flatly.

That brought Celestine Fitzroy to an upright position. She reached for a tan canvas beach bag, pulled out a pack of cigarettes and lit up.

Without being invited, Norah lowered herself into the beach chair next to Celestine's towel. "Great place to live," she remarked, looking around appreciatively. "Except in the winter, I suppose. It must be lonely in the winter."

"I'm not here that much. I travel. I'm an airline stewardess. Of course, you know that."

"Yes, I do."

Norah delved into her handbag and brought out a photograph. "Do you know who this is?"

Celestine Fitzroy squinted, then shaded her eyes; it protected them from the glare and masked her expression at the same time. "Sure. That's . . . Barthelmess. Will Barthelmess. He's running for senator."

"You're interested in politics?"

"No. Whenever there's a celebrity on board there's a buzz among the passengers and the word gets around."

"He's not a big celebrity though, is he? Not somebody everybody recognizes like—Ted Kennedy or even Patrick Moynihan."

"No, not like that," Celestine Fitzroy agreed. "Of course, once he was pointed out to me, I recognized him the next time I saw him. He's very good-looking."

"So he's flown with you more than once."

"Oh, sure."

"How many times?"

She shrugged.

"Alone?"

"Yes, alone. I guess you don't get to take your staff and secret service and all that till you're elected. Unless you've got lots of money, in which case I suppose you'd charter your own plane."

"Mr. Barthelmess's campaign tank is running on empty."

Fitzroy shrugged and handed the photograph back.

"I'd like you to try and recall which of your flights Representative Barthelmess was on."

"That's very hard. I go back and forth so many times."

"Okay, take the last time. When was the last time he flew with you?"

The stewardess bit her lip. "Going in which direction?"

Good question, Norah thought. Smart. "Either."

Fitzroy frowned over it, then gave up. "Sorry."

Was the alibi going to crumble this easily? Norah thought. Could she afford to accept the disclaimer? If she did, she ran the risk of Fitzroy's suddenly remembering later on. If the case went to trial, the stewardess's support of Barthelmess's alibi would be that much more dramatic, and the blow to the case against him that much more devastating. Norah had no choice but to be specific.

"I'm interested in a flight out of New York on May sixth, at nine P.M.

Mr. Barthelmess claims to have been on it. He's confident you'll remember he was on it."

The stewardess pondered. After a few moments, the uncertainty cleared. "Sure! Now I've got it. It was a Saturday, so the schedule's light. He almost missed the flight. That's how I remember. We were all set to separate from the jetway when we got the order to hold for one more passenger, and it turned out to be the congressman."

"Ah . . ." Norah nodded. "You would remember a thing like that, wouldn't you?"

"Sure."

She seemed pleased, Norah thought, and she should be, she'd handled it very well.

"And so would the passengers, of course. The problem is in tracking them down." Norah mused aloud. "For confirmation. Not that I have any doubt; it's a matter of routine." She paused. "The crew! Sure. The crew will remember; the cabin crew and naturally, the flight crew."

Celestine Fitzroy shuddered. In the searing sunshine, her smooth, glowing, tawny skin broke out into goose bumps. She'd made a mistake and she knew it. She had said too much, elaborated when it wasn't necessary.

The mistake of an amateur, Norah thought. "Why don't you tell me the truth?" she urged gently.

But Fitzroy tried to salvage something, tried to make a deal—her evidence in exchange for immunity.

Once, not so long ago, Norah would have rejected it out of hand; now she hesitated, and the words came hard. "I can't make any promises."

But by now Celestine was eager to get rid of the burden. The story gushed out of her.

Flying a regular run to Bogotá, Colombia, she had for over a year been a courier for one of the big drug cartels. At first, her luggage passed unopened through customs, and she could carry drugs in and money out with perfect assurance. She picked up the drugs from an airport locker in one city and delivered them in the same way at the other end. Returning, she carried the money and followed the same procedure. Recruited by a friend, she had never had contact with anybody in the network.

"I was getting nervous." As she said it, Celestine reached for her robe. Though there were no clouds in the sky and what light ocean breeze there was had all but died down, she put it on. "Then my friend who got me the job disappeared. I couldn't find out what happened to her. The word was that she had voluntarily committed herself for treatment. I didn't even know she had a problem. By then, I was having a problem myself—I mean, my luggage was being subjected to spot-checks. I don't know why. Then suddenly, I was switched to the Washington–New York shuttle. Obviously, my usefulness as a courier was over. I was relieved. I didn't hear anything from anybody, so I assumed I was in the clear. Then out of the blue I got this phone call. It was a man. I didn't recognize his voice, and he didn't identify himself. He just told me to make sure I didn't forget Representative Will Barthelmess was a passenger on my nine P.M. flight to Washington on Saturday, May sixth."

"And was he?"

Her hand shook as she buried the glowing tip of the cigarette into the sand. "No."

"Is there anything else you want to tell me?"

"No, except . . . I never touched the stuff. I swear to God."

Norah called on Arenas, Wyler, Neel, and Ochs, the four members of the squad who had been working on the case since the beginning, for a brainstorming session in her office. She presented her reconstruction. They punched holes in it and then helped to plug them. They probed for weaknesses and then helped defend against them.

Simon Wyler was the last holdout. "Maybe we don't need it to make the case, but I'd like to know for my own satisfaction. I'd feel better, okay?" He looked around. "It's about the shooter—how did he get away? No, listen—one minute he's in the middle of the playground spraying bullets at random, and the next he's gone. Vanished. I can accept a man walking around in battle dress without attracting particular attention: it takes a lot more than that to get a second glance in this town. But the guy was carrying a rifle. He couldn't hide it. You say he went up to the apartment, changed his clothes and stashed the gun there. But that's fifteen blocks he was out on the street and we can't find anybody who saw him!"

"So he didn't walk the fifteen blocks," Neel argued.

"What did he do? Take a taxi?" Wyler's irony was heavy.

"We've been taking it as a given that he fired at random," Norah pointed out, "but the indications are contrary. Here's the sequence: he enters the area from First Avenue, guns down Dolores Lopez and strafes the baby carriage. The rest of the bullets go high and into the wall. Obviously, their purpose was to cover his escape. With the first shot, everybody ducked and ran for cover. Who was going to risk getting his head blown off by looking up? All the perp had to do was keep shooting till he got out of the line of vision. Go take another look at the bullet tracks on that wall. They stop at Sixty-eighth in the middle of the block. I'd say he had a car parked close by."

"A rental?" Simon asked.

"What else? And you've just bought yourself the job of tracing it."

"Suppose he used phony ID?"

"He probably did."

Wyler groaned.

"And I agree with you, it would be nice to know how he covered those fifteen blocks. Make us all feel better."

Wyler groaned again and everybody else laughed.

On the basis of the plan that finally evolved, Norah went to Captain Jacoby and once again requested permission to fly down to Mayagüez. She intended to bring Carmen Herrera back with her. Jacoby agreed.

Carmen Herrera, however, was not as easily convinced.

Norah had taken the earliest flight out of Kennedy to San Juan with a fifteen-minute lapse to connect with the local flight to Mayagüez. She made it, and by a few minutes after twelve was sitting on the veranda of the hacienda belonging to Carmen's parents. Looking out, she saw what Randall Tye had seen—a garden of tropical beauty, beyond it at the bottom of the hill scintillating, azure water—and suspected, as he had, where the money for it all came from. The very openness, the absence of a wall or fence was in itself a kind of protection for no one could approach without being seen. Norah had immediately identified the houseman who answered the door as a bodyguard, and where there was one, undoubtedly there were more.

"How long are you going to sit out here in the middle of nowhere with your armed patrol?" she asked.

Carmen Herrera looked off into the distance.

"Why did you pretend the baby was your sister's? Wouldn't it have been easier to pass him off as your husband's?"

Carmen turned her dark, limpid eyes on Norah. "He couldn't have been Juan's. Juan is sterile."

She remembered with sharp clarity Juan's reference to his wife's recent miscarriage. What had seemed a natural remark was now revealed as a pathetic attempt to cover his impotence. A lump rose in Norah's throat. It was Carmen she felt sorry for.

"Did Juan find out the baby was yours? How? From Dolores?"

Carmen's face was twisted with anguish. "She didn't mean to hurt me or the baby. I tried so hard to keep her away from the trade, but she was only a young girl. She saw so much money and it seemed so easy. I know she was tired of always asking for any little thing she wanted. So she went to Juan and made him give her a job."

"You thought it was Juan who killed Dolores and the baby; that's why you gave Randall Tye the information that led him to Juan and the money laundering."

"Yes," she said softly.

"But once Randall revealed the money-laundering scheme, that would be the end of Will Barthelmess's run for the Senate nomination. He'd certainly lose the election. You didn't want that?"

Carmen licked her lips nervously.

"Or did you?" Norah's heart beat faster, as the tangled emotions and desires began to unravel. "In your heart were you afraid of what would happen when he did win?"

Carmen turned her head away.

"Suppose Juan didn't know about the baby?" Norah persisted. "Or if he knew, didn't care? Suppose Juan isn't guilty?" When she saw that Carmen didn't intend to speak, she asked as gently as she could, "Does Barthelmess know about his son?"

Carmen's nod was barely discernible.

Norah had brought a newspaper in which the accounts of the Barthelmess campaign and Judith Barthelmess's suicide were prominent. She now showed it to Carmen. "Judith Barthelmess went to the apartment you shared with Will. She saw the picture of the two of you and the baby."

"I'm sorry about that."

"Come back with me," Norah pleaded. "Find out once and for all what happened."

Carmen Herrera took a deep breath. "Later."

"You mean after the election? That will be too late. You won't have any hold on him then."

There was nothing more Norah could say, no argument she could make. She fell silent and waited.

In a voice that was barely audible, Carmen Herrera asked, "What do you want me to do?"

Chapter

TWENTY

Having agreed to cooperate, Carmen Herrera followed Norah's instructions to the best of her ability. She placed the call to Will Barthelmess using his private number in Washington.

"I have to see you," she said. No need to identify herself; he knew who was calling.

"Not now."

"Yes, now. I miss you. I need you."

"I feel the same way, but we can't afford to meet."

"At the apartment."

"No, not even at the apartment. It's too much of a chance."

"What chance? Judith's gone. You can't use her for an excuse anymore."

"Judith was never an excuse. You know that."

Carmen Herrera rode right over him. "I'm coming in tonight. Meet me at the apartment at eight."

"This is a bad time, I tell you. Darling, please. I'm still in the race, but barely. I can't afford . . . Sweetheart, you've been so understanding and patient. Can't you wait a little longer?"

"No, I can't. I'll be at the apartment at eight. If you don't come, if you're not willing to stand by me . . ."

There was a moment of shocked silence. "What do you mean—stand by you? Carmen, what do you mean?"

"Juan knows. He knows the baby wasn't my sister's, that he was mine. I haven't told him who the father was . . ."

"All right, all right, calm down. I'll meet you, but not at the apartment. Let's see . . ."

"At the airport?" Carmen suggested.

"Yes, all right. What time does your flight come in?"

Carmen Herrera looked to Norah, who was sitting across from her and listening on an extension. She had the answer ready on a slip of paper which she now handed over.

"Pan Am flight 907 due to land at seven-fifteen."

"I'll be there." In Washington, D.C., Will Barthelmess hung up.

So did Carmen Herrera, aka Mrs. Charles Hunt, but not in Mayagüez, P.R., as Barthelmess assumed. She had returned to New York with Lieutenant Mulcahaney and to the apartment, which for nearly two years had been the rendezvous for her and Charles Hunt, aka William Jason Barthelmess.

"Well done, Carmen," Norah told her.

"You are wrong about Will, you know," Carmen repeated as she had many times since she'd agreed to put him to the test. "You'll see." It was herself rather than Norah she wanted to convince.

That was 2:10 in the afternoon.

The call had purposely been placed late enough to rush Barthelmess and to permit him little time to think or to question Carmen's appeal, but early enough so that technicians could install the additional telephone lines and electronic listening devices. Norah hoped that by the time Barthelmess entered the apartment, he would be too agitated to be suspicious.

No action was expected till the flight Carmen was supposed to be on landed. Still, there was no telling what preparations of his own Barthelmess might be making. So Danny Neel and Julius Ochs were posted outside the building on Eighty-third. Simon Wyler remained in the apartment with Carmen Herrera not only to protect her, but to make sure, as the hours dragged by, that anxiety didn't cause her to change her mind and back out. Norah went back to the squad. With Arenas and Tedesco, she reviewed what should take place at the airport. If he intended to meet the plane at Kennedy, Barthelmess would probably be landing himself at LaGuardia no later than six P.M., just in order to have plenty of time to transfer. In case he should jump the gun, Norah sent two detectives to Kennedy early and two to LaGuardia.

By six, she was back in the "Hunt" apartment with sandwiches and coffee for everybody.

"The Pan Am flight is on time," she announced and passed out the food.

Only Carmen had trouble getting the hamburgers down; the others were accustomed to eating under stress; there were plenty of ulcers in the police department. When the meal was finished and the leftovers cleared, there was nothing to do but wait.

At 6:32, the newly installed telephone in the kitchen rang. Everybody jumped. Norah answered. It was Ferdi calling from Kennedy.

"He's here."

At 7:01 Wyler checked the airline and was assured that yes, Flight 907 from San Juan was at that moment coming in for a landing and should be at the arrival gate at 7:08 P.M., seven minutes early.

The next minutes dragged. Everybody in the apartment on Eighty-third visualized the plane taxiing, the impatient passengers standing in the aisle waiting to get off. Finally, the plane would come into its berth, the jetway would be connected, and the passengers would stream through and into the terminal.

There would be no customs or immigration check, nevertheless the DEA took an interest in all flights arriving from the islands and scrutinized the deplaning passengers. To that end, the passengers were herded by a circuitous route to the luggage carousels, where they waited under observation before being permitted to claim their belongings and unite with friends and relatives. That could take a while. By seven-thirty, however, it could be assumed that everyone was on his way home. Not seeing Carmen, Will Barthelmess would be confused, even concerned. Where was she? He might assume a problem with the luggage and allow another ten minutes, but by seven-forty, panic would set in. Could they somehow have missed each other? Maybe she hadn't been on board? Had there been a change of plans? If so, why hadn't she got in touch?

The special phone in the kitchen rang again.

"He's standing at the arrival gate, very confused," Ferdi reported. "The last of the passengers is off and the cleaning crew is boarding. He seems to be trying to decide whether to question the airline personnel."

"We'll put in the page," Norah said and signaled to Wyler in the living room.

He got on the regular phone. Arrangements had been made with the phone company to leave a line to the PA operator at Kennedy open and with the announcer to make the page immediately upon notification. The sound of his voice echoing in the vastness of the terminal could be heard on the line.

"Call for Mr. Charles Hunt. Mr. Charles Hunt please pick up a courtesy telephone."

Wyler handed the receiver to Carmen Herrera.

Several anxious moments passed. Would he answer the page? Then a click and a guarded voice.

"Hello? Who's calling?"

"It's me. Carmen."

"Carmen!" Relief was followed by anger. "Where are you? What's this all about? Why are you paging me? Where are you?"

"I didn't know how else to get hold of you," she answered humbly, as instructed. "I'm at the apartment. I came in on an earlier flight and I didn't know where else to go. I'm sorry, Will."

"Sorry doesn't help."

"Don't talk like that to me, William."

"All right. All right. I apologize."

"There was no space on the later flight," she explained. "I had to take what I could get."

"Sure. Maybe it's just as well. Stay where you are. I'm on my way."

He hung up, so did Carmen, and everybody grinned. The first hurdles had been cleared. Arenas and Tedesco would follow the suspect in from the airport and would advise of any detours or stops en route. In this instance, no news would indeed be good news. Forty minutes later, Norah ordered everybody out to another apartment down the hall, which the tenant had agreed to let them use for a couple of hours.

Fifteen minutes after that, Representative Will Barthelmess rang the doorbell of 9A. He waited and rang a second time. Still no answer and no sound from inside. Annoyed, with an uneasy look around, he fished for a ring of keys in his pocket, selected one, and let himself in. He made sure to close the door firmly behind him before calling.

"Carmen? Carmen! Where are you?"

Silence.

It was then he noted the lights were on everywhere, not only in the living room where he stood, but in the bedroom, bath, even the kitchen. It was a habit of Carmen's; once she turned a light on, she didn't turn it off till either she went to bed or left. From the living room, he looked in the kitchen. A cup of coffee, half full and cold, stood on the kitchen table with an open copy of *People* magazine, to which Carmen was addicted, beside it. Everything indicated she had stepped out for a few minutes—to get cigarettes or milk or some other damn thing,

Barthelmess thought, so whatever was bothering her couldn't be all that serious. He was relieved and annoyed at the same time. He glanced at his watch, then got the step stool and carried it into the bedroom. Opening the closet door, he positioned the stool so that he could reach the suitcase on the top shelf.

He packed what was left of his clothes. Then he went through his bureau drawers and the medicine cabinet for any other indications of his occupancy. Once more he looked at his watch. Twenty minutes had passed since he'd arrived. Where the hell was she? If she didn't show soon, he'd have to just walk out, but God only knew how she'd react to that. He had survived a series of revelations and implications and insinuations on the part of the media. His colleagues in the House were looking askance at him, steering clear. After Judith's suicide, the scandal of an illicit affair would finish him. That had to be avoided at all costs. At all costs, he thought. So he couldn't just walk out, but he could go down to the lobby and leave the suitcase at the desk so she wouldn't see him going out with it. He had it in his hand when the front door opened.

"Going somewhere, Mr. Barthelmess?" Norah Mulcahaney asked.

"Lieutenant! What are you doing here?"

"I might ask you the same thing."

"It's none of your business."

"I think it is. Very much so. I'm afraid I have to read you your rights, Congressman." Reaching into her purse, Norah easily found the plasticized card; she'd had it ready.

"Wait. Hold it. I came to visit a friend. Is there a law against that?"

"A very dear friend? A friend with whom you share this apartment?"

"I don't share this apartment with anybody. I told you, I'm visiting."

"You're not Charles Hunt?"

"Who's Charles Hunt?"

"A short while back you answered an airport page for Charles Hunt." He shook his head, but he also turned pale. "You were observed by two detectives as you answered the page. A recording was made of the conversation and a voice analysis will identify you and the person you were speaking to."

William Jason Barthelmess was a politician, a public speaker and debater, a man used to thinking on his feet, but he couldn't parry this thrust. He did manage to hold his head high while his glittering eyes remained fixed on Norah.

"This apartment is rented in the name of Mrs. Charles Hunt," she went on. "That is the name used by Carmen Herrera. She has admitted it. Now we know you are Mr. Charles Hunt."

He had to clear his throat a couple of times. "All right," he said. "All right. We had an affair. What's the big deal? I'm not the first man in government who ever played around or cheated on his wife. I'm sure you don't need me to name names. Times have changed and the voters are not as tolerant as they used to be. If you make this public, you'll destroy me. My career will be finished. And it won't do you any good. It won't solve your case."

He was shifting the responsibility onto her shoulders, a habit of his, Norah thought. Of course, he was also playing for time.

He became ingratiating. "Anyhow, it's all over between Carmen and me." He indicated the suitcase he still held. "As you can see, I'm clearing out my things."

"Does Carmen know?"

"She knows it's over. She may not want to admit it."

"You should have told your wife it was over. Maybe she'd still be alive."

"You're a real romantic, Lieutenant," he scoffed. "Judith didn't kill herself because I was having an affair with another woman. I don't mean to sound callous, but if that were the reason, she would have done it long ago."

"Are you telling me this is not the first time you've cheated on your wife?" Norah's blue eyes were cold.

"I seem to have offended your sensibilities. The fact is Judith killed herself because she got tangled with the mob. She knew she would be charged with money laundering, convicted, and sent to prison. She couldn't face it." A light gleamed in his eyes. "I'll make you a deal, Lieutenant Mulcahaney. I'll give you the individual who recruited Judith and set up the whole operation, the top boss, if in turn you forget about . . ." He made a sweeping gesture. "If you forget about all of this."

"We already have that information."

"I don't think so. It's not Juan Herrera. Juan is the front. Ralph Dreeben gives the orders."

He'd expected some indication of surprise, but Norah disappointed him.

"Ralph Dreeben concocted the scheme and organized it. A couple of

years ago there was a conference in San Juan on the statehood issue for
Puerto Rico, one of many. Members of the committee who brought
their wives did so at their own expense: it was scrupulously legitimate.
Though he knew I was short of cash, Dreeben specifically suggested I
bring Judith. It was because of her real-estate connections, of course.
He took her aside and explained the scheme. Then he introduced her to
Herrera."

"You knew about it all along? From the start?"

"He also introduced me to Carmen."

Norah was genuinely shocked. She didn't know what to say.

"Lieutenant, my first campaign for the state assembly was run on the
notion that right makes might. I made no commitments, no promises; I
accepted no favors if I even suspected there were strings attached. And
I lost. The system under which we operate, Lieutenant, penalizes hon-
esty. I learned that whatever good intentions you may have, whatever
ideas for reform, before you can implement them, *you have to get
elected.*"

"So all the while your wife agonized that you might find out where
the money for your campaign was coming from and turn on her in
righteous indignation, you knew!" Norah exclaimed. "You knew all the
details because you were having an affair with the drug dealer's wife. In
the past, Judith had closed her eyes to your infidelities, but this time the
betrayal went too deep. She'd sacrificed her integrity to protect yours
only to find out you didn't have any."

"Spare me your moral indignation, Lieutenant. I have enough on
Ralph Dreeben to make a very big bust for you. Do you want it or
not?"

"You actually intend to go on with the campaign?"

"I do and I intend to win. Why are you so set against me?"

He was serious, Norah marveled. He really wanted to know. "Ralph
Dreeben may be corrupt and he may have corrupted others, but he
didn't kill anybody."

Barthelmess's eyes glittered malevolently. "I'd be careful what accu-
sations I make, Lieutenant. Even police officers can be sued. When
Randall Tye died I was up in the skies over Washington, D.C. I have an
alibi, as you well know."

"Your wife had the alibi, not you," Norah retorted. There was no
accomplice, never had been, she thought; she'd been wrong about that.

However, the scenario she'd envisaged worked as well with Will in Judith's place.

"When you and Randall parted, you headed for the departure gate, but you didn't board the flight. You doubled back and caught up with him in the parking lot. On some pretext or other you got him to let you into the car. By now, the mickey you'd slipped into his drink was starting to take effect. You kept him talking till he passed out. Then you pushed him aside and took the wheel. You drove along the highway till you found a secluded spot and you pulled over and administered the drug."

"I respect your feelings about Randall Tye, Lieutenant. I understand you want to clear your lover's name, but this is pure imagination."

Norah didn't pay attention; another seemingly irrelevant fact suddenly made sense, was even significant. "Your next concern was to get back to the airport and catch the next flight out. It was a long walk and you might be seen, even offered a ride and recognized! The risk was too great. So you turned the car around and drove back as near as you dared."

The guarded look, the pinched lips, told Norah she'd hit it.

"You keep ignoring my alibi. The stewardess on the nine o'clock will vouch for me. Why don't you talk to her?"

"I already have. She's changed her testimony."

"Why should she do that?"

"Because she lied the first time."

"Who says?"

Norah went over to the coffee table, directing her voice toward a small bowl of flowers. "Would you like to answer that, Mrs. Herrera?"

Before Barthelmess could pull himself together, the front door opened and Carmen Herrera, accompanied by Detective Wyler, walked in. Barthelmess regarded her with eyes that were cold and almost hostile.

"Would you like to answer the congressman's question?" Norah asked again.

Carmen Herrera tried. She looked up into Barthelmess's face, but she couldn't go through with it.

"Carmen," Norah urged gently. "You must speak."

Sensing that he was still in the game, that he still had a chance, Will Barthelmess made a complete change in attitude and directed the full battery of his charm on the distraught woman. *"Carmencita. Querida.*

This whole thing is entrapment. A trick. Don't you see it? We've been set up. What I said earlier was to save us both. I didn't mean it. I promise you as soon as the election is over, we'll be married. I swear it."

There were tears in Carmen Herrera's eyes. She wanted desperately to believe him; Norah could see it. He still had power over her. He was a fighter, resourceful, wily, devious, and devoid of conscience. Carmen was his victim as much as any of the others.

Norah, however, wasn't finished either. She still had one hole card. She pointed to the suitcase he had never once let out of his hand.

"What've you got in there?"

"Nothing much. Personal belongings. Papers I brought along to read on the plane. There's no end to the amount of reading we have to do."

The attempt at lightness fell flat.

"Do you mind opening it?"

"Yes, I do. I've told you there are official documents inside."

"Surely you're not carrying around classified information? Never mind. We won't look at the papers. Hand over the case."

"No, you have no right."

"We have a search warrant." She brought it out and showed it to him. "It covers everything in this apartment."

"I brought the suitcase with me from Washington."

"Is that so? Mrs. Herrera," Norah appealed to the dazed woman. "Have you ever seen this suitcase before?"

"It looks like one he keeps on the top shelf of the closet."

"I own more than one suitcase, for God's sake."

"Detective Wyler, would you step into the bedroom and see if the congressman's other suitcase is in there?"

Wyler was gone a matter of moments. When he came back, he merely shook his head.

"I want to call my lawyer," Barthelmess said.

"After you open the suitcase."

At Norah's nod, Wyler stepped forward and Barthelmess had little choice but to let him have the case. The detective opened it. It was neatly packed. Wyler carefully set aside the folded shirts and shorts till he uncovered the army uniform and the automatic rifle.

Carmen Herrera blanched. "You killed them?" She stared at him in terrible awe. "You gunned them down—Dolores and my baby? All this time I've been thinking it was Juan. Juan was so jealous. He couldn't give me a child, but he never would have allowed me to keep one I'd had by another man. I thought Juan had killed them, but it was you." Her voice was low, throbbing with anguish. Then came the full realization. "You meant to kill me."

He flushed. He couldn't speak.

"You mistook Dolores for me."

"You don't know what you're saying."

"She was my height, wore her hair like me, and was always borrowing my clothes. That day she was wearing my white pants suit. Saturday was my day for taking the baby out. You knew that. Dressed in my clothes and wheeling the baby, you thought she was me."

"Carmen, for God's sake, that's crazy."

"Juan wouldn't have mistaken her for me."

"You don't know what you're saying."

"I wasn't good enough to be your wife. I wasn't good enough to be the Senator's Lady."

He groaned.

"Madre de Dios, I knew that," Carmen went on. "Deep in my heart, don't you think I knew? I knew it would never happen. You would never leave your wife and marry me, not because you loved Judith so much, not because you'd been childhood sweethearts, but because she was useful to you. I'm Puerto Rican, the wife of a drug dealer, I'd only drag you down. You were afraid I'd reveal our relationship and create a scandal. It would cost you the election. So you decided to get rid of me."

Barthelmess could only shake his head.

"I would never have forced you to marry me. I would never have revealed our relationship. I would never have exposed you to shame. You didn't have to kill them—Dolores and the baby . . . our baby. How could you do it? How could you murder your own child?"

"Women do it every day. They call it abortion."

With a scream, she flung herself at him, sobbing convulsively, beating him with her fists. It took both Wyler and Norah to pull her away.

"You wanted to know about his alibi for Randall Tye's death?" she asked Norah. "He doesn't have one. He wasn't on that nine o'clock flight. The stewardess did lie. She lied because Ralph Dreeben went to Juan. Juan was her connection and he ordered her to lie. Cocaine will buy just about anything."

Even an election. The words were not spoken, but they were heard throughout the room.

* * *

While Wyler and Arenas escorted the suspect through the booking
and arraignment process, Norah notified the U.S. Attorney.

Al Virgilius complimented Lieutenant Mulcahaney. He didn't try to
argue priorities with regard to the NYPD's arrest of Representative
Barthelmess, though very likely he would take it up with the Manhattan DA. Not that he'd get very far, Norah thought: Homicide took
precedence over any other charge he might ultimately make and he
knew it. He did advise the lieutenant to stay clear of Ralph Dreeben.
Dreeben was his.

That was okay with Norah, but "He's an accessory before and after
the fact," she pointed out.

"I'm not likely to forget it. Rest assured, he's going to be prosecuted
to the full extent of the law." Al Virgilius was not particularly skilled
nor interested in the slow process of investigation. He had his own team
of detectives, but as long as he got the facts, he didn't really care who
had done the legwork. He was brilliant in the courtroom. "Trust me,
Norah. He's going to get everything that's coming to him—in spades."

Next, Norah tried to contact Jim Felix, but he was still away. Manny
Jacoby, however, left his dinner and came to the station house as fast as
he could.

"You should have informed me," he muttered after hearing her out.

"I'm sorry, Captain."

"No, you're not."

That startled her. "You're right, Captain," she admitted. "But I
couldn't think of any other way. I figured the sequence like this: Carmen deliberately put Randall on to the money-laundering scheme, be-
lieving her husband, Juan, was guilty of the murder of Dolores and the
baby.

"Randall followed the lead to Judith Barthelmess, visiting her in her
Georgetown office late Friday afternoon, and returning to New York
that evening. He tried to contact Ralph Dreeben, but Dreeben was
attending a testimonial dinner, so he went home, and the next morning,
Saturday morning, drove out to Dreeben's house.

"Immediately after the interview, Dreeben contacted Barthelmess
and warned him Randall was headed his way. Randall knew too much.
He had to be silenced. Dreeben, who had masterminded the whole
setup from the beginning, even to promoting an affair between the congressman and Carmen Herrera, had a very strong suspicion that

Barthelmess had already bloodied his hands and he didn't want to be a part of anything like that. So he worked out a way to counteract the threat, supplied Barthelmess with the heroin, which I assumed he got from Herrera, and arranged for Barthelmess's alibi."

Norah paused. "It's my opinion that Dreeben only meant to put Randall in a compromising situation. He meant for him to be found unconscious in the car, with the empty syringe beside him and visible tracks on his arm: *in flagrante,* so to speak. The public might be inclined to be tolerant of his first transgression; that hadn't been his fault, after all, but they would not forgive the second. Their compassion would have been used up. Tye would be disgraced; his credibility destroyed. I don't think Ralph Dreeben ever meant to go beyond that, certainly not for Randall to be killed. In fact, he was trying to avoid it."

Jacoby formed a silent whistle.

"Maybe Barthelmess made a mistake," Norah went on. "Maybe he administered an overdose by accident. But the amount was so large." She shook her head. "It was massive."

"I'm sorry, Norah."

"I think Barthelmess saw a chance to shut Randall up once and for all, and he couldn't resist it. If he'd made a deal with Randall, he wouldn't have needed to go back to Randall's place and make sure there was nothing there to incriminate him." She fought back the tears. "We had no proof of any of this, so we had to go after Barthelmess for the flea-market shooting."

"You had the rifle," Jacoby pointed out. "You'd found the rifle on the first toss of the Hunt apartment earlier this week."

"Yes sir, and under the comparison microscope the bullets were a match to those recovered from the bodies of the two victims. But who did the rifle belong to? Naturally, it wasn't licensed. There were no prints. Logically, it belonged to one of the occupants of the apartment —Mr. or Mrs. Charles Hunt. Mrs. Hunt had already been identified as Carmen Herrera, so we needed to get William Barthelmess to acknowledge himself as Charles Hunt. Once he responded to the page at the airport, he incriminated himself at least to the extent of being involved in an illicit affair. That didn't convict him of murder. We needed to catch him with the weapon in his possession. So we put the rifle back."

Expecting an objection, Norah paused, but Jacoby remained silent.

"But would even that be enough? Would anyone believe that William Barthelmess, a charming, attractive member of the House of Representatives and candidate for the U.S. Senate nomination, had put on an army uniform, disguised himself with a beard, walked into a crowd of women and children and opened fire? We had to show motive, not reasonable, but overwhelming, incontrovertible. To do that, we had to convince Carmen Herrera to turn against him. It wasn't enough to tell her that her lover had never intended to divorce his childhood sweetheart and marry her. If we'd told Carmen he killed Dolores and the baby in mistake for her, she would have been outraged. She would have used every means and every ingenuity to defend him. We had to let her figure it out for herself."

Jacoby nodded.

"I should have advised you what we were up to, but to tell you the truth we were kind of playing it by ear." (Translation: If I'd told you, you would have shut us down.)

"Sometimes, you have to go on instinct," Jacoby admitted.

Norah gaped.

"But watch it," he warned. "Next time the breaks might not go your way." (Translation: Then you'll be the one to take the heat.)

That was more like it, Norah thought and grinned.

It was nearly midnight when Norah returned to her own office. Time to go home, she thought. Why rush? Nobody was waiting for her. Nobody was there to wonder why she was late, what had happened, or to care, not even a pet—a cat or a dog or a canary, no creature dependent on her. A stack of DD5s had accumulated on her desk. She sat down, but she didn't touch them. They could wait. She could go through them tomorrow, and if she didn't—somebody else would.

She dropped her head in her hands.

She had cleared Randall's name, and though she still had no hard evidence that Barthelmess was his killer, she had identified him as the flea-market shooter and linked the two cases. She'd accomplished what she'd set out to do, but there was little satisfaction in it. On the contrary, she felt drained. Tomorrow loomed ahead without purpose or promise, along with the day after that, and the weeks and the months.

Time passed. She didn't bother to check her watch when the tap sounded at her door. Danny Neel was there.

"Buy you a drink, Lieutenant?"

She started to say no, then thought—why not?

They walked the few blocks to Vittorio's. She and Joe had courted there, those long years ago. It was where Jim Felix had thrown the party to celebrate her promotion to Lieutenant. It was one of the recognized hangouts, but she didn't drop by often anymore. Nevertheless, Vittorio himself went behind the bar to pour the white wine she always ordered.

"Congratulations, Lieutenant. I hear you made a big bust." He set the wine in front of her. "On the house."

The door opened and Nicholas Tedesco came in. Then Julius Ochs. "Hi, Lieut," they called and then came over and took stools at the bar.

One by one, the men of the Fourth Homicide Division drifted in—those just off duty came from the station house and those who had worked earlier shifts came from home. They ranged themselves around her.